ME, MOP, AND THE MOONDANCE KID

ME, MOP, AND THE MOONDANCE KID

Walter Dean Myers

Illustrated by
Rodney Pate

**Delacorte
Press**

To the Little Leaguers

Published by
Delacorte Press
The Bantam Doubleday Dell Publishing Group, Inc.
666 Fifth Avenue
New York, New York 10103

Text copyright © 1988 by Walter Dean Myers
Illustrations copyright © 1988 by Rodney Pate

The trademark Delacorte Press® is registered in the U.S.
Patent and Trademark Office.

Library of Congress Cataloging in Publication Data

Myers, Walter Dean, [date of birth]
  Me, Mop, and the Moondance Kid / by Walter Dean
Myers; illustrated by Rodney Pate.
        p.   cm.
Summary: Although adoption has taken them out of the
institution where they grew up, eleven-year-old T.J. and
his younger brother Moondance remain involved with
their friend Mop's relentless attempts to become adopted
herself and to wreak revenge on their baseball rivals the
obnoxious Eagles.
  ISBN 0-440-50065-6
  [1. Baseball—Fiction. 2. Adoption—Fiction. 3. Afro-
Americans—Fiction. I. Pate, Rodney, ill. II. Title.
PZ7.M992Me 1988
[Fic]—dc19   88-6503
                                                    CIP
                                                     AC

Manufactured in the United States of America
November 1988
10 9 8 7 6 5 4 3 2 1
BG

ou gotta help me, T.J. I'm *desperate*!"

"I don't think it's going to work."

"It's gonna work!"

"I don't know . . ."

"The mumps are a sign, T.J. I just know Donald's mumps are a sign straight from heaven!"

"Sister Carmelita tell you that?"

"She don't have to tell me everything. I know a sign when I see one, and them mumps are a sign!"

"Okay, I'll see what I can do," I said.

"And while you're seeing about it, just remember who it was saved Moondance from drowning in Lincoln Park, okay?"

"I told you I'd see about it," I said. "I got to get home now. You be cool."

"I can't be cool until I'm sprung from here and you know that, T.J."

"Yeah. I know that," I said.

I started walking down the Boulevard, away from the Dominican Academy, but I knew Mop was watching me. I could feel her eyes burning right into my back. When I reached Kensington, I turned around and she was still standing there outside the gates, just the way I knew she would be, staring at me.

I know how she felt. The Dominican Academy is part school and part a home for kids without parents to take care of them. I knew all about the Academy because me and my brother, the Moondance Kid, had spent most of our lives there. We were just adopted six months ago, but Mop hasn't been adopted yet.

Mom was making supper when I got home, and the Moondance Kid was doing his homework. It was May and it was getting hard to do your homework. The days were long and so warm that you just wanted to get outside and do things.

"How did your day go?" Mom asked.

"Fine," I said. I sat on the couch next to where Moondance was sitting and started thinking about Mop some more.

"Is there anything wrong?" Mom asked.

"No," I said. "I was just thinking about a friend."

"Probably Mop," Moondance said. "You're always thinking about her."

"Why don't you dry up and blow away!" I said.

"Are you sure everything's all right, T.J.?" Mom asked.

"Sure," I said, squeezing out a smile.

Sometimes I forget how easily Mom worries. I think when she and my new father first adopted me, she was more worried than we were. All you have to be is quiet around her for two minutes and she starts asking if everything is okay. I like it, though. I'm eleven and I spent eight years in the Dominican Academy, so I'm glad to be adopted. No, it was better than just glad, it was truly juicy.

Oh, also, I do always think about Mop. Mop is the kind of girl you have to think about because she's real nice and everything, but she'll get you into more trouble than you can ever imagine.

Take for instance how she saved Moondance from being drowned. She saved him, that's right. But guess who was the one who almost got him drowned? Sister Carmelita had taken us all down to Lincoln Park and everybody was playing volleyball except Mop and Moondance. The next thing I knew was that I heard screaming, and there were Moondance and Mop in the middle of the lake hanging on to a wooden plank. She'd told him they could use the plank like a raft and sail across the lake. That's why she had to save him.

Okay, there's this Little League baseball team called the Elks. The coach of the Elks is a guy named Jim Kennedy. I met him when I was at the Academy because he and his wife came around and looked at some kids. They didn't have any kids of their own and they were thinking of adopting one. What Mop wanted me to do was to tell Jim to go to the Dominican Academy and ask to have her on the team. The nuns are really cool about getting the kids involved in community things.

When I got out to the park the next day I told Jim all about Mop.

"And you say she's a catcher?" Jim asked.

"Yeah, she's real good too," I answered.

"How big is she?" Jim was hitting fly balls to the fielders and he knocked one out toward Moondance. I watched as Moondance circled under the ball, almost caught it, and then chased it back toward the fence.

"She's not too tall," I said. "But she's strong. She could beat just about every boy in Dominican at arm wrestling."

"And you say she caught for the Dominican team?" He hit another long lazy fly to where four of the Elks were standing, they all called for it, and it hit Brian Fay on the foot.

"She caught for us and she was good," I said.

"I didn't even know Dominican had a Little League team," Jim said.

"It wasn't exactly Little League," I said, "but it was a team."

"Well, anyway, with Donald coming down with the mumps we need a catcher. I'll give her a try. What's her full name?"

That's how easy it was to get Mop on the Elks. Maybe Donald Wheeler's coming down with the mumps was a sign, like Mop said. To tell the truth, the Elks weren't the greatest team in the world. Nobody really wants to be on the Elks. Mike Nieto, our first baseman, said that Donald got the mumps on purpose just so he didn't have to play with us. But I didn't believe that.

The first day of practice with Mop went okay. Not great, mind you, but okay. She didn't hit the ball too good and Brian got on her case.

"How come we have to get another girl?" he asked. "We already got Jennifer who's slow and Chrissie who's terrible. Now we got three on our team."

"How would you like me to break your face into nineteen little pieces?" Mop said, going right up to Brian.

"You and what army?" Brian said. But he didn't say it too strong because Mop was right in his face and she looked like she meant what she was saying.

"Come on." Jim raised his voice as he stepped between them. "This is supposed to be a team. Anybody that can't play as a team can't play for the Elks!"

Mop sure could catch the ball. When she got behind the plate with the catcher's mask on you couldn't tell if she was a boy or a girl. You couldn't even tell when she talked, because she has a really deep voice for a girl. Kind of gravelly too.

"Listen up, guys!" Jim said as we put the bats and bases in the equipment bag after practice. "We have our first game Wednesday at four-thirty. I want everybody here by four o'clock so we can take infield practice. Evans, you'll be our regular catcher and Mop can be the backup."

"I don't want to catch." Evans's whole name was Jesse Evans but everybody just called him by his last name. I don't know why. He was always getting mad at somebody, but it was funny because he had this voice like the chipmunk you see on television on Saturday mornings. When he got really mad his voice went even higher. "She can catch if she wants."

Me and Moondance walked Mop back to Dominican.

"See, that's what I told you," Mop said. "Nobody wants to be a catcher because they're all afraid of the ball. That's why I knew I was going to make the team."

"What's this plan you got?" Moondance asked.

"Okay, it's real simple," Mop said. "I'm going to be catching, see? Then the coach starts to think I'm terrific, mostly because I am. And who's the assistant coach?"

"Mrs. Kennedy."

"Right. And who do you think was coming to the Academy and looking me over and thinking about adopting me?"

"You?"

"No, they talked to some boy, but once Mrs. Kennedy asked Sister Carmelita how old I was. I know that 'cause Sister Carmelita tells me everything."

"So big deal."

"Anyway." Mop took a deep breath the way she does sometimes when she's really talking fast. "I'll be behind the plate catching and throwing runners out at second base and everything and they'll be wondering how come I'm so good and everything. Then one day there's going to be a pop foul and I'll jump up and throw off the mask and catch the pop foul. When I catch it, I turn to Mr. Kennedy and give him a little smile. Not too big a smile because I don't want them to think I'm trying to butter them up or anything but a little smile so they know I'm friendly.

"Then . . ." She took another deep breath. "He's going to say to his wife, or maybe to himself if she don't come, 'You know, that's the girl I've been thinking of adopting out of Dominican. Wow, she's a good catcher. I was wondering if I should adopt a boy, but she's just as good, maybe even better, so I'll run right down tomorrow and take out the papers!'"

"How you know he's gonna say all that?" Moondance asked.

"Did I know I was going to be playing for the Elks?"

"Did you?" Moondance asked.

"Yeah, sure I did," Mop answered.

"I think you got it made now," I said. "All you got to do is not mess up in the games or anything."

We had reached the big front door of Dominican. Mop opened it and stuck one leg inside.

"That's not the whole trouble," Mop said. "Sister Marianne said that since not too many kids are going to the school now, they're going to close it down. They said it costs too much. She said they'll probably close down Dominican or maybe combine it with St. Aedan's. The rest of the kids will go out to Riverhead, which is about a trillion miles away."

"You too?" I asked Mop.

"I will if I don't get this Kennedy dude to adopt me soon," she said. "Sister Carmelita thinks he's interested, and she don't know what's holding him up."

"What did Sister Marianne say?"

"Same thing she always says." Mop folded her hands in front of her chest the way Sister Marianne always did. "The Good Lord moves in mysterious ways. . . ."

"His wonders to perform." I finished the sentence.

"Wish He'd check me out pretty soon," Mop said.

Most of the kids at the Academy are young. Mop and me were just about the oldest. When kids get to be eleven or twelve, they're usually sent out to another home. I would have been sent out to Riverhead except for Moondance. They like to keep brothers together. Me and Mop have known each other a long time, so that's how we got to be such good friends. That's how she got that name, Mop, too.

My real name is Tommy Jackson. When I was nine another kid came to the Academy with the same name. At first I thought it was pretty cool, but he didn't like it. And he was tough enough to do something about it too.

"You either change your name," he said. "Or I'm going to break your nose."

Did I tell you I'm not too tough? Well, I'm not. And when the new Tommy Jackson told me to change my name, I thought maybe I would do it. But then I found out you just can't go and change your name.

"You got to go to court and everything," I told the new Tommy. I had to look up when I spoke to him.

"You got two problems," he said, holding his fist about an inch from my nose. "Your name and my fist! You better come up with something quick!"

That's when I started calling myself T.J. T.J. stood for Tommy Jackson, but it sounded different. When I told Billy—that's Moondance's real name—that he should call me 'T.J.,' he wanted a new name too.

"We'll call you 'B.J.,' " I said.

Only thing was, he didn't like it. So he started calling himself the Moondance Kid. He had seen a movie called *Butch Cassidy and the Sundance Kid.* He liked "Sundance Kid," but since that had already been used he started calling himself Moondance.

Now Mop heard everybody calling me T.J. and my brother the Moondance Kid, and she asked how come they were calling us that. I didn't want to say that I was scared of the new Tommy, so I told her that it was really cool to have a name like T.J. or Moondance. So she wanted a new name too.

"We can call you 'O.P.,' " Moondance said.

Olivia Parrish made this face like she just bit down on a bad pistachio nut. "That's stupid!"

"Why's it stupid?" I asked.

" 'Cause!"

"How about the Starlight Girl?" I asked.

She liked that a lot and almost decided to use it when Snotty-nosed Eddie Hurly asked her what she was going to use when she grew up and wasn't a girl anymore.

"I think we ought to go back to O.P.," I said.

"Then it's got to be Miss O.P.," she said.

It wasn't long until we got from Miss O.P. to Mop, which was the first letters of Miss Olivia Parrish.

Mop is really okay. I like girls just as much as I like boys, anyway. Mop knows things about people, too. If you're sad, she'll know it before anybody else. Or if you're thinking about something secret, she can usually figure it out. She says it's because she's smart. Maybe. I think she just guesses lucky. But she did figure out when I was going to get adopted.

We had been playing volleyball last March and Mop was mad because she lost. She *always* gets mad if she loses. That's the way she is.

"You stink!" she said to Snotty Eddie.

"You stink worse than me." Snotty Eddie wiped off his face with the palm of his hand. I hated it when he did that. "You stink and you're a double stink!"

Now, I know that normally Mop wouldn't let Snotty Eddie get away with that, even if he was only nine and she was eleven. She would give him a knuckle sandwich right in the lip. But she just gave him a bad look instead and waved a hand at him.

"You get lost, you triple-stink boogie burger!" she said. "I got some business to talk with T.J."

Snotty Eddie stuck his tongue out at Mop and took off for the boys' dorm.

"He's probably going to tell Sister Marianne you called him a boogie burger!" I said.

"She knows he's a boogie burger," Mop said, chewing on her gum. "Nuns ain't dumb!"

"What did you want to talk about?"

"You see that guy and the woman talking to Moondance before?" she asked. "You want some gum?"

"Yeah."

"So what you think?"

"I think I want some gum," I said.

"I mean about them talking to Moondance?" she asked. She was fishing around her pocket for the gum.

"I don't know," I said, watching as she found a Chiclet, brushed it off, and handed it to me.

"How long you had this gum in your pocket, Mop?"

"Kiss it up to God," she said. "That's the third time I seen them here. Twice they were in the office talking to Sister Marianne. I thought they were going to be cottage parents or something. But they were talking to Moondance today and that's got to mean something. I bet they're going to talk to you next."

"Could be," I said, kissing the gum up to God so He could clean it up or something before I put it in my mouth.

"Go ask him what they was talking about," she said.

I went to look for Moondance in the boys' dorm. On the way I took the gum out and took a fuzzball off it. God was only good for germs, not fuzzballs.

Moondance wasn't in the dorm. I asked Anthony Tindal if he had seen him.

"Yeah, he's talking to some people in the gym," he said. "I think he's been talking to them for about a year!"

That's the way Anthony talked. If something was bigger than him, he would say it was bigger than a house. If it lasted more than a few minutes, he would say it was a year. Things like that.

"You going to go in and see what they talking about?" Anthony asked when he saw me lie down on my cot.

"I don't care what they're talking about."

That was a lie. Not a real lie, but not exactly the truth either. I mean, I didn't have to cross my fingers or anything, but I did care a little about what they were talking about. I mean, if they were talking about adopting somebody, then I cared. If they were just talking about the Academy, I didn't care. Sometimes people came and asked how we liked being at the Academy and stuff like that.

The only thing was that if they were talking about adopting somebody, I wondered if they were thinking of adopting Moondance. And if they were thinking about adopting him, were they thinking about adopting me too.

Sometimes me and Moondance used to look in the mirror and try to figure out what our regular parents looked like. He was too young to remember them. I wasn't too young, only I didn't remember them anyway. In fact, the only thing I can really remember is thinking about them after the police came to my old school and said that they had been in an accident. They must have been pretty good-looking because I'm pretty good-looking. Moondance isn't ugly, but his eyes are too big. Makes him look a little like a seal. You ever see a seal with them big eyes looking right at you?

The people that adopted us looked okay too. Their last name was Williams.

I asked, "What we supposed to call you"—

"—Whatever you want to." Mrs. Williams said it so fast that Moondance jumped a little.

"How about you?" I asked Mr. Williams.

He looked at me, then he looked at his wife, and hunched his shoulders.

"How come we just don't call you Mom and Dad?" Moondance asked.

"That would be fine," Mrs. Williams said.

Mr. Williams smiled and I figured that's what he wanted us to call him. That was cool, too, because I didn't want to go around calling him Mr. Williams all the time.

My new mom was pretty, but my new dad was just okay-looking. He didn't have too much hair on the top of his head, but he had a lot on the sides. He told us that being bald ran in his family. He was kind of fat too.

He always liked to tell these corny jokes. One joke he told was about how a boy orange and a girl orange were hanging from a tree. The girl orange was ripe and fell off the tree. The boy orange wasn't ripe, but he fell right behind her. The girl orange asked the boy orange how come he fell off the tree.

"You know what the boy orange said?" Dad asked.

"What?" Moondance asked.

"He said, 'Because you are so a-peeling,' " Dad said.

"Oh." That's what Moondance said.

"That's a joke." Dad nodded his head up and down. Then he said it again, talking real slow so we wouldn't miss anything. "Because-you-are-so-a-peeling!"

"Oh," Moondance said again.

"Don't you think that's funny?" Dad looked at me.

"Yeah" was the only thing I could think of saying.

I don't know where he gets his jokes, but he has a new one every day. You know who laughs at them? Mom. It's like her job or something. She has this little nervous laugh and she always laughs even before he finishes telling the joke. Maybe it is her job.

Mop got to go to the supermarket with us a week before our first game. Mop gets to come over to our house a lot. That's because the nuns keep talking about how all the kids from the Academy are family forever. Sometimes Mop stays over the weekend and sometimes she just stays for supper and Dad drives her back to the Academy. I don't like that. Going back to the Academy is a little sad. Not a lot, because the Academy is all right, but it's not like having your own home and your own parents and everything.

So Mop was going to have dinner with us on a Saturday and we were out shopping. Mom could cook just about everything that counted. I don't know if she could cook broccoli, but broccoli didn't count. We were going to have spaghetti and meatballs. Moondance loved spaghetti and meatballs. Me too.

"Did you know that Marco Polo got spaghetti from China?" Mop asks Mom.

"Yes, I did," Mom said. (Oops, forgot to tell you that Mom is a schoolteacher and knows just about everything. Dad works in an office.)

"Did you know that when he was in China, he rode on a camel?" Mop asked.

"No, I didn't," Mom said.

Mop gave me a look with her head leaning back, the way she always does when she thinks she's being real smart. Then, when Mom went into another aisle to look for oregano, Mop asked how come she didn't know that Marco Polo rode on a camel when he was in China.

"Don't you worry about it," I said. "Whoever adopts you probably won't even know what spaghetti is."

"If they know enough to adopt me, it means they know a lot," Mop said.

I was just about ready to tell Mop that anybody who adopted her probably didn't even know what a meatball was, when guess who comes down the aisle pushing a whole cart full of cat food? Mrs. Kennedy.

"Hi, guys!" she said. Her teeth are so straight across, you could put a ruler right on them and it would touch all the way. "Are you shopping alone?"

"No," Moondance said. "My mom is shopping with us."

Just then Mom comes up with a box of cereal, the kind that's supposed to be good for you but that tastes like you're eating wood.

"I'm the assistant coach of their Little League team," Mrs. Kennedy tells Mom.

"I'm Mrs. Williams," Mom said.

"T.J. looks just like you," Mrs. Kennedy said.

"Thank you," Mom said. She's still holding the cereal in her hand and I don't know why she don't just put it in the cart.

"We're looking forward to doing well this year," Mrs. Kennedy said. "If everybody works hard."

"We're going to work so hard, it'll knock your socks off!" Mop said. "You just wait and see."

"I hope so," Mrs. Kennedy said. "The Elks haven't

won more than one game per season in the last four years!"

"Some teams just seem to have a lot of bad luck," Mom said.

"Bad luck my foot!" Mrs. Kennedy said. "Joe Treaster's the main reason if you ask me."

"Joe Treaster?" Mom finally put the cereal in the cart.

"He gets all the good players," Mrs. Kennedy said. "I think he scouts them right from the nursery. What poor Jim and the Elks get are the leftovers."

"I ain't no leftover!" Mop said.

"Mrs. Kennedy didn't mean that you were, Mop," Mom said.

"No, I didn't . . . really I didn't." Mrs. Kennedy put her hand out toward Mop and then pulled it back. "I'm sure you're going to do quite well, Mop."

"Maybe even quite great!" Mop said.

"You're really different, aren't you?" Mrs. Kennedy shook her head. "Look, I have to run. We have guests for dinner. I hope I'll be seeing you at the games. Mrs. . . .Williams, was it?"

I could have sworn Mrs. Kennedy had left even before Mom answered. I turned toward Mop and saw that she had this mean look on her face. Her bottom lip was up over her top on one side and her eyes were squinched.

"She better watch out who she's calling a leftover!" she said.

Our first game was with the Lions. There are only seven teams in the league and all of them have names of animals or birds. There are the Eagles, the Lions, the Pumas, the Bears, the Hawks, the Colts, and us, the Elks.

"Hey, Jim." Brian was lacing up his sneakers. "We gonna win today?"

"I hope so," Jim said. "You listen to me and play like I tell you and we should win."

"We can't beat the Lions," Chrissie said. "We can't beat anybody!"

"Not with a stupid girl like you playing," Brian said.

Chrissie has this weird little smile she gives everybody. She gave it to Brian with her eyes crossed.

"Okay, let's have an infield practice," Jim called out. "Everybody in the infield! Everybody!"

Brian was a pretty good hitter and he hit the ball to the rest of us in infield practice. I stood near third base and Mop was near me.

"Hey, T.J.," she called, "tell me if I do anything wrong."

"Yeah."

The first ball that came to Mop went right between her legs. Mop gave me a look and a shrug.

"That could happen to anybody," she said.

Brian hit another ball to her and it hopped over her glove.

"What am I doing wrong?" she asked me.

"You gotta be smooth," I said.

Brian kept hitting the ball on the ground and most of the time we missed it. The Lions started showing up and I was getting pretty nervous. It was my first year of Little League ball, which wasn't too bad. But Mom had said that Dad played real baseball. I mean he played for a real major league team once. Honest. She said that if I was good enough, he could probably get me a tryout for a major league team when I got older. And I was pretty good already.

Mop missed everything that came to her and Brian called her a turkey and Jim made him stop.

"We play," Jim said, "as a team. Is that understood?"

Everybody said yeah and then we sat down and watched the Lions warm up.

"Hey, T.J., are you real good?" Mike asked.

"Yeah," I said.

"How good?"

"One time a major league scout came and saw me play and wanted to know who I was," I said.

"Did not!"

"It wasn't a big thing," I said. "Soon as he saw I was just a kid he wasn't interested anymore."

"Oh."

Jim had me playing third base, which I liked. He put

Mop in the outfield along with Chrissie and Moondance. Usually they put the young kids in the outfield.

Let me tell you who the whole team was.

Jim Kennedy, he's the coach. He's okay.

Then there's Brian, he's strong-looking with red hair and freckles.

Next there's Evans. He's mostly skinny. Also, he's left-handed. Maybe most of the time he's left-handed. It depends on whether he remembers to bring his glove or not. If he doesn't, then he plays with whatever glove he finds. I think he's not too sure which he is.

Joey DeLea is the smallest guy on the team. He's about four foot tall and he's always getting into a fight.

Jennifer Lee is chunky. She looks smart, mainly because she wears glasses, but she always says stupid things.

Then there's Chrissie Testor. She's kind of nice-looking, but mostly she doesn't want to get hit by the ball. Sometimes when the ball comes to her, she closes her eyes.

Then there's Frank Law. He never says anything, and he looks a little mean.

Then there's Lo Vinh. His first name is Xieng. We call him Lo Vinh. He's Vietnamese and a pretty nice kid. He can't catch, but he's a pretty nice kid just the same.

Mike Nieto is funny. He announces everything he does. If a ball comes to him, he makes believe he's a television announcer and says things like ". . . there's a hard smash to Mike. He's up with it, makes a long throw to first base . . . In time!"

Even if he misses the ball, he says that.

Then there's Mop and Moondance and last of all there's me. I guess I'm the star of the team.

Last there's Marla Kennedy, the coach's wife. She's a little like him, except a lot tougher. Maybe not even tougher, maybe just when she tells you to do something, you know she means it. And you know something else? Mop can't even talk to her or come near her without getting nervous.

Marla is cool. She wants us to call her by her first name. She's tall for a girl. Even for a woman. She's taller than my Mom and she always talks a little funny. Not funny weird but funny sort of ha-ha. Not *really* ha-ha but sort of ha-ha. You want a for-instance? For instance, when I first joined the team and Jim told me to go speak to Marla about getting a uniform, right? So I go over to her and ask her can I have a uniform. You know what she says?

"Would you like one made of cotton or would you like one made of cotton candy?"

"You can't make a uniform out of cotton candy," I said.

"Then I guess you're stuck with plain, ordinary old cotton," she said.

She even looked sad when she said it, as if maybe you could make a uniform out of cotton candy. A uniform made out of cotton candy would really be stupid, especially if it rained.

The Lions had a really fast pitcher and he struck out our first three batters, Joey, Frank, and Mop. When Mop struck out, she got mad and threw her helmet down and Brian told Jim. That's one of the rules, you can't throw anything if you're mad.

"If you throw anything down on the ground, you're on the bench!" Jim said. "And if you throw anything up, you'd better catch it before it hits the ground."

Jim gave Mop one more chance because it was her first game.

The first Lion walked. Joey was pitching and he kept giving the umpire dirty looks. Then the next Lion hit a ground ball right to me. You know what happened? The ball must have hit something, because it didn't bounce up. It went right under my glove. Swoosh! Just like that.

You know what I think? I think that sometimes worms crawl around under the ground and make it soft so the ball doesn't bounce right. The Lion got to second base.

Two more Lions got good hits and then they had two runs. The next guy struck out and the next hit a pop-up to Brian. Brian always caught pop-ups.

It must have been catching, because the next guy hit a pop-up toward me.

"There's a *long* fly ball to T.J.," I could hear Mike announcing. "He's under it . . . he's under it . . . and . . . it's off his glove!"

I think the wind must have got it or something. Because it was headed straight for my glove and then it missed it. I don't know how it could do that.

Somebody was yelling for me to throw the ball to first base. I picked it up and saw that the guy who had hit the ball was just starting to run.

Did I tell you about my elbow? I think there's something funny in it, because sometimes when I throw a ball I throw it straight but then it curves away from who I was throwing it to. Maybe I should have been a pitcher.

◆ 23

We lost the game, 18 to 5. The only Elks who got any hits were Brian and Frank. Brian got four hits. One ball almost went over the fence.

I didn't get a hit mostly because of Jim's angles. Jim believes in playing everything by the right angle. So he figures out on a slide rule which angle you should hit at. He told us all to hit down on the ball at a thirty-degree angle.

"That way you won't pop the ball up and they'll have to throw you out at first base," he said.

I didn't think that was such a good idea. It might have worked for Joey because he was small, or it might have worked for Mike because he was tall. But it couldn't work for everybody, right? I know it didn't work for me.

"You stink!" That was what Mop said after the game.

Can you imagine her saying that to me, the star of the team?

"So, how did you like our first game?" Marla asked, as she gathered up the equipment.

"It was okay," I said.

"What did you think, Mop?"

"It was okay," Mop answered.

"I think we could all use a little more practice," Marla said. "Tomorrow at three-thirty, okay?"

One good thing about playing Little League baseball that nobody talks about is that you get to talk to grown-ups like they're regular people. At least most of us can. Mop is kind of afraid to talk to Marla. She keeps thinking she's going to say something wrong.

"You gotta talk to her," I said. "She's the assistant coach."

"It's the way she looks at me all the time," Mop said. "You know what I mean? Sometimes when I'm not even near her I look over at her and she's looking right at me!"

"That's 'cause you're on the team," Moondance said. "That's what coaches do."

"She's sizing me up," Mop said. "One time I was watching television and this announcer comes on and they were looking at the ball players. They look at one guy and the announcer says he looks like a hitter. That's what she's doing. She wants to know if I look like a hitter or something."

"She can see if you're a hitter during the games," I said. "She don't have to look at you when you're just standing around."

"I don't know how she expects me to hit when she keeps looking at me that way."

That was true. When somebody looks at you a lot, it's hard to do what you're doing. It's like their eyeballs are making you move in slow motion or something.

"Jim don't look at you that way," I said.

"She's checking me out for her husband," Mop said. "He's still trying to make up his mind if he wants to adopt me or not. It's like the Yankees. When they want to see somebody, they send a scout to check them out."

"So what you gonna do?"

"If I could talk to her, I think I could get her on my side," Mop said. "You know, maybe get her to tell me what she's looking for and stuff."

"So talk to her," I said.

"I would if she'd only stop looking at me."

When me and Moondance got home we found it was Family Discussion Day. We're the only family I know who have names for different days. We have House Day, that's when we clean the house. We have Church Day, which is Sunday, and that's cool. We have Family Activity Day when we all have to do something together, and we have Family Discussion Day. The only day I really like is House Day, because after we clean the house we usually have pizza and sometimes we go out bowling. It's like we give ourselves an award.

Moondance likes Family Discussion Day because of the rules. I think Mom made up the rules. Anyway, they go like this: Everybody gets to talk for five minutes at the beginning of the conversation without being interrupted. I hate that. Dad, he can talk forever. Mom can talk a long time too. Moondance talks and even though he's not talking about what everybody else is talking about, we all have to listen. He loves that. One time we were talking about peace in the world and he started talking about comic books because he had one that had something in it about peace in the world. Mostly it was about Spider-Man, though, and Moondance told us all about how Spider-Man wanted peace. But first he had to tell us about how he got to be Spider-Man, which I knew already so I wasn't interested.

Today we started talking about health and good nutrition. Mom started off talking about how important it was to eat a good, well-balanced diet. She talked about different food groups. Then it was Moondance's turn.

"I like to eat different food groups," he said. "Mostly groups of peas and groups of carrots."

"That's not what your mother means when she says food groups," Dad says.

Then Mom gave him a look and he gave her a look back. He wasn't supposed to interrupt Moondance. Those were the rules for the first part of the conversation. Moondance noticed the looks and he kept on talking about different groups he liked to eat.

"Groups of rice, and groups of string beans, and groups of spaghettis," Moondance went on.

Dad was getting mad, but it wasn't his turn yet.

It was my turn next, and I asked if I could talk about something I had heard at the Academy and Mom said yes.

"You can talk about anything you want at Family Discussions," she said. "Even if it doesn't exactly fit our topic."

She gave Dad a look.

"Well, this kid who used to be at the Academy said that he thought the best food was junk food. He said that kids ate junk food and then adults got them to eat regular food and not so much junk food.

"Adults say that you should eat regular food that's good for you, but it's mostly adults who get sick all the time. That's what this kid said. He said old people hardly ever eat junk food and they get real sick. So maybe junk food is better for you than other food. That's all I have to say."

"The reason that adults get sick more than kids is that they're older," Dad said. "It doesn't make any difference what you eat. When you get older your body doesn't respond as well as it does when you're very young."

◆ 27

"And eating junk food," Moondance said.

You're not supposed to get mad at Family Discussions, but Dad went into the living room and started reading the paper. That was about the same as getting mad, if you know Dad. Mom was trying to explain to us how eating good food when you're young helps to keep you healthy when you're older. When she finished, she asked if we had any questions.

Moondance wanted to add that he had left off groups of pies from his list. I don't think she wanted to answer him.

wo bad things happened the next day. I hate it when two bad things happen on the same day. The first thing that happened was that Mop found out that Taffy, the llama at the Academy, had to be shipped to a zoo or back to the llama farm it had come from.

Hey, did I tell you about Taffy?

Somebody had donated some money to the Academy about a year ago. Some of the money was used to replace a stained-glass pane that had been broken for years. With the rest of the money Sister Carmelita, Sister Felicia, and Sister Belinda were allowed to go to California to visit a school out there. They came back with lots of pictures. One of them was taken on a ranch where they raised llamas. Sister Carmelita had really liked the llamas, and talked about how cute and friendly they were.

Then one day a crate arrived at the Academy with a small llama in it. We called it Taffy, because it was taffy-colored. Taffy arrived at Dominican just three days before Moondance and me left to live with the Williams family.

"I love Taffy more than anything in the whole world except you and Moondance," Mop said. "And maybe Sister Carmelita. I just can't stand her being put in a zoo.

◆ 29

It's like she's got to go to jail and didn't even do anything. She won't get a trial or nothing."

"What zoo's she going to?" I asked.

"They don't even know," Mop said. "Sister Marianne said they were going to try to find a zoo around here but if they can't they might have to send her all the way out to San Diego, California!"

That was bad, but then another bad thing happened. Mr. Treaster, the coach of the Eagles, showed up. This is one guy I didn't like. He had a big head and these light-colored sneaky-looking eyes and a way of smiling when he talked, like he was laughing at you or something.

"You got a bunch of real athletes here," he said to Marla.

Marla looked at him and gave him a quick little smile. "Okay, team, infield practice!"

Jim worked during the day. Marla was a teacher and she usually ran practice except on weekends.

I was on first base and the first ball that came to me went right over my glove. I thought I had it, but it hopped funny at the last minute.

"Come on, T.J.," Marla called out to me. "You have to watch the ball."

She hit the next ball to me and I really watched it good. I didn't catch it, but I watched it good. What happened was that I was watching it so hard that I didn't move my glove fast enough and it hit the side of the glove and went over toward where Mop was standing.

"T.J., you stink!" Mop yelled.

"Mop!" Marla called out to her. "On this team we encourage each other, okay?"

Mop didn't say anything.

Now Marla hit the next ball to me too. I don't know why she did that. I didn't catch the first two balls. The way I figured it, if I was doing good, I could practice that. But if I was doing bad, I shouldn't practice because I was just practicing to be bad.

The next ball went through my legs.

"Get the glove down, T.J.!"

The next time I got my glove down, but the ball bounced high and I missed it. I didn't feel bad about that one because Marla had told me to get my glove down, so it was her fault.

Treaster was sitting on the bench and he was laughing. Marla hit a ball toward Mop and she got it and threw it to Mike, who was covering first.

"Good play, Mop!" Marla called out.

Mop was the only one that really looked good. Every time we'd make a mistake, Mr. Treaster would smile and shake his head. After a while as soon as somebody missed a ball or threw it wrong, we'd look over at him to see what he was doing. Marla looked at him a lot, too, and I could tell she wasn't happy with him sitting there watching us.

Marla called us all in and said that the regular practice was over. Then she asked who wanted to practice pitching. Moondance said that he wanted to practice pitching and Mop said that she would catch.

"You can't catch!" Evans said.

"Evans Shmevans, shut up!" Jennifer made a face.

Mop put on the catching gear and Marla and I stood behind the fence. Mr. Treaster came over and stood near us.

"You have to be a lot tougher with these kids," he said. "You have to handle them! That's what coaching's all about!"

"We'll be okay," Marla said.

Moondance started pitching. The first pitch went right over Mop's glove and went bang! into the fence. Marla and I jumped back.

"You think you'll win a game this year?" Mr. Treaster asked.

Marla turned to him, but he had already started walking away.

I watched Moondance pitch five more balls to Mop and they all went over her head.

"I told you she can't catch!" Evans called out.

"He throws too high," Brian said.

That was right. Moondance was throwing the ball too high, but he was throwing it just about as fast as the pitcher on the Lions. One time he threw it in the dirt and it bounced up and hit Mop in the mask. Marla ran around the backstop to see if Mop was okay.

"Don't sweat it, Coach," Mop said. "I'm cool."

We got home and ate and then Dad came home. Moondance and I were lying on the floor watching television with our gloves on.

"You guys want to go out and throw the ball around a little?" he asked.

"Okay," I said.

Big mistake.

I told you Dad used to play baseball in the pros. Mom said he only played for three years because he hurt his knee, but one of those years he was in the major leagues. I figured he probably didn't do that good, though, because they never made a baseball card with his picture on it or anything.

We went over to the ballpark and he started throwing the ball to us. Only he threw hard. I mean he threw it harder than Brian ever dreamed of throwing it and Brian can throw hard. But you know what happened? Moondance could catch it. Moondance thought it was funny that Dad should throw so hard.

"You throw harder than anybody on the team!" Moondance said.

"You have to know how to handle the ball," Dad said, throwing the ball to me. "Let's see your arm."

I knew what he meant. He meant for me to throw the ball to him hard. I wound up and threw it and it didn't reach him. He started to tell me how to stand and stuff. Which leg to put in front of the other, that kind of thing. I did it a little, but it didn't help too much.

Then he threw the ball to Moondance and Moondance caught it and threw it back hard. Dad had to jump to get it, but it smacked into his glove and he said something about Moondance having a real arm.

I didn't feel terrible. Not super terrible anyway. Maybe just a little terrible. When I was at the Academy, I used to dream about being adopted and having a father who would take me out to play baseball. Now I had one and maybe I wasn't that good. Or then, maybe I was. Maybe I was just having a bad day.

But what was a surprise was how Moondance could throw the ball so hard and how most of the time he caught the ball when Dad threw it to him. Moondance had hardly ever played ball at the Academy, so I don't know where he got all his practice from. Maybe what I was thinking before was right. Maybe I was getting too much practice being bad.

When we got back to the house, Mom started talking about how Dad had read this interesting article on nutrition.

"Why don't you tell the boys about it?" Mom said.

But he didn't want to talk about nutrition. What he wanted to talk about was playing ball. He started telling us stories about how he had played ball when he was our age. He made it sound like a lot of fun.

I figured out why Mr. Treaster had come to our practice. Our next game was with the Eagles, the team he coached.

"We have to change our hitting angle for this game," Jim said. He had his slide rule out. "The Eagles have better infielders than outfielders, so we're going to try to hit the ball over their infields at a . . . twenty-degree upward angle. Everybody got that?"

We all had it after he showed us how the bat was supposed to look when we swung. Too bad he didn't tell the Eagles that.

The Eagles were all just like Mr. Treaster. They yelled at us when we made a mistake and they yelled at each other. Sometimes they even swore. When they swore, I looked over at Mr. Treaster to see if he was going to say anything, but he didn't.

The first inning wasn't too bad. We didn't get any hits

but Brian got a walk. Then they got up and they only got two runs. Frank was pitching for us and he looked pretty good.

The second inning was bad. We got out one-two-three and the Eagles were laughing it up. They had this one guy, they called him Rocky, who would stand on first base and yell, "Swing!" every time one of us got up. Marla went over to the umpire and told him to make the guy stop. The umpire made him stop, but then their whole team would make believe they were swinging bats.

Rocky was the first guy up in the bottom of the second.

"He swings and hits a long drive into deep left field . . ." Mike was announcing the game again. ". . . It's going, it's going, it's *gone!*"

They scored eleven more runs before we got up again.

I played okay. I didn't get any hits or anything but I only made two errors in the field. The first ball was a hard smash that bounced right off my leg and went against the fence near the Eagles' dugout. Talk about hurt. Everybody was yelling for me to go get the ball but I was sitting on third base rubbing my ankle.

Mop went and got the ball. Then Marla and Jim came over and looked at my leg. I guess it was okay. I looked over at the seats where the parents were and I saw Mom standing and looking toward me. Dad had his arms folded and was looking the other way.

The next ball that came my way was a slow roller. I was glad to see that ball coming so slowly. I ran in after it, but my foot got to the ball before the glove did and I kicked it. The first thing I did was to look at Dad. He was shaking his head.

We lost against the Eagles, right? So guess what happened? Sister Marianne was there and she's just like happy all over. I think she loves losing better than winning. After the game she even went with a bunch of us to Jerry's Pizza Den.

"Well, well, well!" she said. She kind of puffed herself up so that she looked like a pigeon. "Now didn't the Lord give us a great day today!"

"Yes, Sister Marianne," Mop said. She was talking to Sister Marianne but was still giving me dirty looks.

"I think this great day deserves a special pizza," Sister Marianne said.

She always did that. When you lost something or hurt yourself, she always thought you should celebrate it with a pizza or a soda or something. Then when you won something, you were supposed to sit around and not think it was so hot.

"Sometimes," she said as we settled down around two tables they had pushed together, "the Lord works in mysterious ways."

"That's right," Mom said. She was patting me on the hand because she knew I felt bad about losing.

"Did you know, Mrs. Williams," Sister Marianne went on, "that Saint Sebastian suffered the pain of arrows and humiliation?"

"Oh," Mom said, "did he?"

"Why, yes, he did," Sister Marianne said. "And we all know that those real pains from those very real arrows were more severe than the loss of a mere baseball game."

"That's true," Mom said.

"Who was he fighting, Indians?" Brian asked.

"Infidels!" Sister Marianne said. "He was fighting against the godless infidels!"

Jerry came over and we ordered sausage pizza as usual. Brian wanted onions on his, but Jerry said he couldn't have them unless everyone had them. I think Brian just wanted onions to show that he was grown or something.

"I really wanted to beat those guys," Brian said. "Especially that Rocky, he's such a bigmouth."

"It's only your second game," Mom said. "You'll get better."

"If we got any worser, we'd have to lose two games at a time." Mop folded a napkin and then stuck her finger in it to make it look like a wedding doll.

"What do you think Saint Sebastian would think if he lost one game like this?" Sister Marianne asked.

"I think he would have been pissed off!" Brian said. "Especially after he got shot by the arrows and everything."

"I don't think that's the kind of language you should be using, young man." Sister Marianne raised both her eyebrows the way she did sometimes. "And Saint Sebastian took his pain and his ordeal gladly because he did it for God."

"He got stuck with arrows and he liked it?" Brian asked.

"So, when is your next practice?" Sister Marianne turned toward me.

"Tomorrow, I think," I answered.

Just then I saw Marla coming into the pizza shop. I didn't want to see her. I thought she was just going to say I stunk like Mop did.

"Hi, Mrs. Williams, Sister." She sat down with us. "Mind if I join you?"

"We played lousy, right?" Brian said.

"You could have played better," Marla said. "That's what practices are for."

The pizza came and everybody took a piece. Mop dropped hers, sauce side down, right on her lap. Moondance was the first to laugh and then I started laughing and then Marla laughed. Mop got mad, stood up, and went into the bathroom.

"I hope she isn't upset," Mom said.

"She's usually the first to laugh at herself," Sister Marianne said. "I think they're taking the losing too hard. I was just telling them about the ordeals of Sebastian . . ."

"Who?" Marla was looking at the menu as she talked to Sister Marianne.

"He's this guy she knows who likes to get stuck with arrows," Brian said.

"Oh, *Saint* Sebastian!" Marla said.

"You know him too?" Brian asked.

"Saint Sebastian lived many, many years ago," Sister Marianne said. "But his lesson of sacrifice stays with us even today. Sometimes those who lose a great deal and still keep their chins up are rewarded beyond their greatest expectations. In Sebastian's case he became a saint."

"The Mets almost became saints once," Marla said.

Sister Marianne's eyes went up toward the ceiling and she took a sip of water.

Mop still hadn't come out of the bathroom, so Marla

went in to see if she was okay. Then Brian started talking about what team we could beat.

"Most teams can take us easy," he said. "But we'll get the Eagles before the end of the season."

"We should have it so the winner plays the Red Sox or somebody like that," Moondance said.

"You gotta be crazy," Brian said. "The Red Sox would wipe us out and they wouldn't even notice it. Maybe we could take the Padres if T.J. would catch the ball sometime."

"I caught the ball," I said.

I don't know why I said that because I never caught the ball once in the game.

"You what?" Brian's whole face twisted.

"I think he means he stopped it from going into the outfield once," Mom said.

"Yeah, he stopped it from going into the outfield all right," Brian said. "Only he kicked it right off the field!"

I was going to say something dumb. I don't know what I was going to say, but I knew it was going to be something dumb because I always said something dumb when I felt dumb. Lucky for me, just then Marla and Mop came out of the bathroom. I took one look at Mop and knew she had been crying. I looked at Marla and it looked as if she had been crying too.

"Is everything all right?" Mom asked.

Marla kind of smiled and shook her head.

We didn't talk much after that, except for Brian asking Sister Marianne if she was a coach.

"No, I'm a Sister of Charity. That's a nun."

"You don't look like a nun," Brian said. "Aren't you supposed to be wearing a uniform or something?"

"You're not supposed to be asking a nun what she wears, stupid!" Mop said.

"How'd you like your face broke in more pieces than it is now?" Brian pushed Mop's elbow off the table.

Whack!

Mop gave him a shot in the head and then they started wrestling and fell on the floor.

Jerry came over and separated them and we all left.

You know what I didn't want to do? I didn't want to go home and see Dad. I felt a little bit like Mop did about doing good on the Elks. About having my parents think I was good and all. Funny thing was, I didn't even know I felt like that until I was going in the front door.

"Hi, Dad, we lost."

"Sorry to hear that," he said.

"Did you lose a lot of games when you were my age?" I asked.

"No," he said.

I watched the news while Mom made dinner. We were having leftovers and there was a choice of what we could have. I had beef stew and Moondance and Dad had chicken. Mom said she wasn't hungry.

"You know, T.J., even if the ball did hit you, it wouldn't hurt that much," Dad said, looking up from his plate.

"It'd hurt some," I said.

"Are you afraid of the ball?"

"No."

"I think you must be," he said.

"He *said* he's not afraid of the ball," Mom said.

"Hmm!" Dad's jaw tightened a little.

"You ever hear of a guy who liked to get shot with arrows?" Moondance asked. "He was a saint."

"Sister Marianne from the Academy was telling the boys about Saint Sebastian," Mom said. "And how winning or losing a game of Little League baseball isn't all that important really."

"Hmm!" Dad's jaw tightened a lot.

I went to see Mop at the Academy the next day. The way I figured, the team had more than enough players. If I dropped off, it wouldn't really matter.

"I'm thinking about quitting myself," she said. "I even thought about running away."

"Like you did before?" I asked.

"You mean just to the corner?" Mop shook her head. "I mean the whole megillah. Maybe I'll go to China and get married or something. Or maybe to California."

"How come?"

"I don't know, I just got a bad feeling," she said.

You could see it all over her. Her voice was low and she talked down at her hands.

"Did Marla say something bad to you in the bathroom?"

"No."

"What happened?"

"I don't know." She sniffed a little and pushed on her nose. "Soon's she came in I felt kind of funny—like I always do around her. You remember what I told you about the way she watches me?"

"Yeah."

"Well, that's it. She looks at me and then I get all nervous. I dropped that stupid pizza on myself and then I went into the bathroom and all I could do was—you gonna tell anybody?"

"Who me? No."

"You do and I'll wipe you up!"

"I'm not gonna tell anybody!"

"I just started crying and carrying on. Then she come in and said everything was okay and that we'd beat the Eagles after a while. I wanted to say something to her. You know, something cool, like how I knew we were really gonna kick the Eagles' butts or something. All I could do was boohoo all over the place. She probably thinks I'm a nut case."

"You're not really going to run away, are you?"

"I don't have the nerve," she said.

"Maybe we'll beat the Eagles," I said. "Who knows."

"We gotta come in at least second," Mop said. "I found out that the team that comes in first plays the team that comes in second for the championship."

"If we can't beat them in the regular games, we won't be able to beat them in the play-offs," I said.

"T.J., we gotta beat them," Mop said. "We stick together and we'll do it, too. You just wait and see."

I was just about to split from the Academy when I ran into Sister Margaret. She tells me to get her a cold glass of water. When you see Sister Margaret, she always tells you to do something. It didn't make any difference that I was adopted and don't live at the Academy anymore. Not with Sister Margaret.

"And don't put your finger in it to see how cold it is," she said.

Mop went with me down to the kitchen. Sister Carmelita was there with a new kid. She told us his name was Artemis and then he left.

"What kind of name is Artemis?" Mop asked.

"He's a nice boy," Sister Carmelita said. "Maybe later, when he gets used to this place, I'll bring him out for Little League ball."

"You making tea?"

Sister Carmelita had a large pot of water on the stove. It was just starting to bubble.

"Nope, I'm getting out of trouble," she said. "I'm using hot water to get out of hot water."

"What happened now?" Sister Carmelita was the youngest nun at the Academy, and always getting into trouble.

"You remember yesterday the Little Choir was supposed to sing at Mass and they didn't show up?"

"Right," Mop said.

"Well, who do you think was sitting in the front row with her hands folded in her lap instead of bringing the Little Choir to Mass."

"You."

"You got it, baby."

"So what you doing now?"

"Now I am going to surprise Sister Marianne by cleaning all the good glasses. They're crystal, but you couldn't tell because they're so grimy. Nobody's really cleaned them for a long time."

They didn't look that bad to me, but I had seen them

prettier. At Christmas, or when a big shot like a bishop or somebody came to the Academy, Sister Marianne used to put them out.

"So I'm using hot water to get out of hot water," Sister Carmelita said as she took pot holders to lift the boiling water. "This hot water will loosen the grease. Then I will use elbow grease to remove the rest. Stand back!"

She poured the hot water onto the crystal.

It made a nice sound. You know what it sounded like? The first notes of that song about "My Favorite Things." Sometimes when they play that song, they start it off with bells. This wasn't bells, it was the sound of the crystal breaking into little pieces. Sister Carmelita was in big trouble again.

The next time I saw Sister Carmelita, she was in exile or something. Me, Moondance, and Brian are on the field throwing the ball around and waiting for Mop. Mop comes and I see Sister Carmelita is with her. She said Sister Marianne keeps sending her on errands out of the Academy.

"What did she say when she saw the good glasses were broken?" I asked.

"She was so mad, she fell right down on her knees and started praying!" Sister Carmelita said.

"Right there on the spot?"

"Right there on the spot!" Sister Carmelita said. "She turned red and everything!"

"So what did you do?" I asked.

"I got right down next to her and told God I didn't

mean to break her crystal and for Him to keep that in mind when He listened to her."

"Then what happened?"

"Then she got up and just walked away. I don't mind, though." Sister Carmelita said. "I think she really likes me."

"You better watch out she don't shoot you with some arrows and make you a saint!" Brian said.

id I tell you that Moondance had a secret? The secret is his bear. The bear's brown and about eight inches high and he's not fuzzy anymore. In fact, I don't even know if he was ever fuzzy. Dinky looks like he might have been fuzzy once, though. Dinky, that's the bear's name.

Moondance has always had that bear. Even back when we used to call Moondance by his real name, Billy, he had the bear. Neither of us remembered where he got Dinky from and it didn't matter a lot. But he loved him. He was a little ashamed of loving him too. You know, a kid his age loving a bear and all. I liked the bear too. I didn't love him the way Moondance did, but he had been with us for a long time.

I got home about four o'clock and Moondance was really upset.

"Dinky's in the toilet."

"How can a bear be in the toilet?" I asked. "A bear can't pee or nothing. At least a toy bear can't."

"I dropped him in the toilet."

"How come?"

"I had him in the bathroom washing him," Moondance said. "And Mom started to open the door. I jumped and he fell in the toilet."

"Yeah?"

"Then I flushed the toilet."

"How come you flushed it if Dinky was in there?"

"So Mom would think I was using the toilet."

"Mom came in the bathroom?"

"No, soon as she saw I was in there she closed the door real quick and started saying how she was sorry and everything."

"So he's flushed down the drain?"

"Yeah, except it's stopped up," Moondance said, looking real pitiful. "Mom said not to worry about it because Dad would fix it when he got home."

"Oh."

"You think you could fix it?"

I knew Moondance wouldn't want Dad to know it was Dinky that was down in the toilet. I started for the bathroom and Mom told me the toilet was stopped up.

"If you don't have to . . . I mean, I guess you do have to . . ." she said. She had this worried look on her face.

I nodded and went in.

Soon as the door was closed, I lifted the toilet seat. The whole toilet was just about filled with water. I didn't know what to do. There was a thing on the wall that held paper cups and I took one of them and dipped some of the water out and dumped it in the sink. I didn't know what else to do, so I kept dipping the water out. You know what happened? When I had dipped most of it out, the toilet made a funny noise.

Gollub!

That's the way it sounded. The water made a little funny noise and up popped Dinky's arm! I grabbed it and pulled for all I was worth. It tore a little bit, but the head came up next. I held it by the head and the arm. I didn't want to hold Dinky just by the head because I didn't want his head to pop off.

One more pull and he was out of the toilet. Soggy, and a little wet, but he was out.

I rinsed him off real quick in the sink, took an undershirt from the dirty-clothes hamper, and wrapped him up in it. Then I wrapped him in a towel and left.

I gave him to Moondance. "Sorry about his arm," I said.

Moondance smiled this nice little smile he has sometimes. Man, that's a nice little smile he has. Makes me so glad he's my brother. Really.

"Moondance!" It was Mom calling.

Moondance stashed Dinky in the back of the closet where he usually keeps him and we went out to the kitchen.

"You want to help me fix supper?"

"Okay," Moondance said.

"I have to go to the bathroom," I said.

"You were just in the bathroom."

"I got to go again."

"Is everything all right?"

"Yeah."

"The toilet's still stopped up, isn't it?"

"I don't think so," I said.

Mom gave me one of those is-something-strange-going-on looks and went into the bathroom. She flushed the toilet and it worked fine.

She came out and gave Moondance a look and Moondance gave her a smile. Then she shrugged and went back to finishing supper.

That night just before I went to sleep, or maybe it was just after I went to sleep and he was waking me up, Moondance came to my bed and shook me.

"What's the matter?" I asked.

"Thanks a lot for saving Dinky," he said.

"We had to save Dinky," I said. "He's your best friend."

"No," he said. "You're my best friend. Dinky's my second-best friend."

That was a cool thing for Moondance to say. Really.

So the team is on the playing field with Sister Carmelita the next day and we're throwing the ball around a little and talking a lot, the way we usually do, when this guy Peaches comes over to us.

First time me and Moondance saw him was when we were playing football in the park last fall. He's a wino. I don't know why they call them winos. Sister Carmelita once tried to teach us some Spanish and she said that in Spanish the names of boys or masculine things end in *o*. Maybe that's why they called him a wino, because he was a man.

"What y'all doin'?" he asks.

"Fixing to go to the moon," Brian said. "You want to come?"

"Don't you be fresh-mouthing me, boy," Peaches said. " 'Cause I don't take no fresh-mouthing!"

"This is our Little League team," Sister Carmelita said. "We're practicing."

"I used to be one of the best ball players there is," Peaches said. "You know what they used to call me? The Alabama Peach!"

"The what?" Moondance looked at Peaches as if he didn't really believe him.

"The Alabama Peach! They used to have this white guy they called the Georgia Peach and they used to call me the Alabama Peach!"

"Ty Cobb!" Sister Carmelita said.

"You knowed that white boy?" Peaches asked.

"I've read about him," Sister Carmelita answered.

"Here let me show you how to—"

"We don't need you to show us nothin'!" Brian said. Peaches had reached for Brian's bat and Brian snatched it away from him.

"Why don't you split, man?" Mop said. "You don't look like you can teach anybody nothing."

"Aw, I could teach you plenty," Peaches said. He waved his hand at us and started away.

"Would you teach me how to hit?" Sister Carmelita called after him.

"You gotta be kidding!" Brian looked at Sister Carmelita with his face pushed forward and his hands on his hips.

"I'll teach you," Peaches said. "Let me take my coat off here a minute."

He went over to the benches near the field and took off

the dirty old suit jacket he was wearing. We watched him as he folded it carefully and laid it on the bench.

"Yo! Nun lady!" Brian went up to Sister Carmelita. "He's a wino!"

"He's right," Mop said.

"He's a human being," Sister Carmelita said. "One of God's creatures. Now, is there anyone else who would like him to help them?"

"Yeah, okay," I said.

I didn't really want Peaches to help me, but I kind of felt sorry for him. I couldn't tell how old he was, really, but I knew he was old. And I knew he looked kind of thrown away too. I had felt like that before.

"You stand right over here," Peaches said. "Fix your feet like I got mine fixed."

I stood at the plate and placed my feet the way he had his. Then he took the bat that Brian had dropped on the ground, gave it to me, and asked me if I was ready.

"Yeah."

"Okay, when I throw you the ball you keep your eye right on it, but make sure you don't swing the bat until the ball get to you."

He threw the ball. It was high but I swung anyway. I just missed it by this much.

"You swinging too soon!" he said. "Wait till the ball get right up on you and then you gotta swing quick!"

He threw the ball and I missed it again.

"Oh, great, he's teaching you a lot, T.J.," Brian said.

I missed three more balls and Peaches kept telling me to do this and do that. Then I hit a ball and it bounced right back to him.

"Best hit you had all season, T.J.," Mop called out.

I gave her a look and then missed the next three balls.

"You gettin' closer!" Peaches called out.

I threw the bat down. Brian was right.

"I'll try it!" Sister Carmelita picked the bat up.

"Me and T.J. are gonna go play catch," Brian said.

We started off to one side. Moondance came with us and Mop stayed behind.

Crack!

Me and Brian turned around at the same time. We saw the ball go flying through the air and land almost at the fence.

"That's the way to do it!" Peaches said. "That's the way!"

Moondance went over and got the ball and threw it back to them. Peaches did this funny little windup and pitched the ball to Sister Carmelita again.

Crack!

The ball shot over the infield out toward us. Brian tried to flag it down, but by the time he got his glove up it was too late. The ball rolled all the way to the fence. I went over and got it.

"Let's see that ball," Brian said.

He took it, looked at it, and then put it in his pocket. He took out another ball he had brought with him and threw it to Peaches. The ball went right to Peaches. Peaches tried to catch it but dropped it when it hit his hand. He shook his hand a little and gave Brian a mean look for throwing it so hard.

Brian just smiled.

Peaches turned, did his funny little windup, and pitched the ball again to Sister Carmelita.

Crack!

You didn't even have to turn around to know it was gone. I mean *g-o-n-e.* Over the fence!

"That was an official Little League ball," Brian said.

By the time we got the ball and brought it back, Peaches was putting his little dirty coat back on.

"She learn real good," he said. "Yeah, she all right. Y'all have her on your team and you be okay."

"I was telling Mr. Peaches that we'd better have some infield practice now and that maybe he could help us with hitting another day."

"Yeah, maybe," Brian said. He was really looking at Peaches hard. "Maybe."

Peaches did more of a shuffle than a regular walk and I watched him as he shuffled out of the park and down the street.

We were getting ready to have infield practice when Jim showed up with the rest of the team. Moondance started telling him about Peaches, but he wasn't interested. He had brought along a ball of string and he gave me one end of it and told me to stand at home plate. Then he held the other end of it and went out to shortstop. He held it as high as he could and then told everybody to jump up and touch it.

Evans and Mike were the only ones who could touch the string where Jim held it. Then Jim got a box from his car and stood on that and held the end of the string up. No one could touch it then.

"That's the angle we have to hit the ball at," he said. "That way it's right over the infield for a base hit."

You could tell he was proud of that piece of string. He made us take turns standing on the box and holding the string up while the rest of us hit the ball.

You know who came by to watch us practice? If you're thinking Mr. Treaster from the Eagles, you're right.

"Why don't you get some ribbons for those girls!" he shouted out.

Everybody was mad at him. Really. He was standing near the fence and Marla went over and stood right in front of him.

"Why don't you worry about your own team!" she said.

"I got ball players," Mr. Treaster said. "I don't have to worry about them."

Mike got up and touched the string with his bat. Then Jim threw the ball and Mike missed it. But he hit the string that Mop was almost holding. Actually, she had tied it to her finger and when Mike hit it she fell off the box. Naturally, Mr. Treaster laughed. I laughed, too, a little.

"You know what I would like to do to him?" Brian said. "I would like to punch him right in the nose."

"I don't think I could approve of that," Sister Carmelita said.

The whole practice was ruined.

"Suppose we just stuck an arrow in his rear end and made him a saint like that Sebastian dude?" Brian said.

As we packed the bases and things up, Sister Carmelita asked if any of us wanted to help her distribute food to the needy that weekend. Nobody volunteered. We were all too down. Before I left, I asked Sister Carmelita was she good in arithmetic when she went to school.

"Not bad," she said. "Why do you ask?"

"Just wondered," I said.

I figured she was. That's why she could hit the ball so well. She knew all about those angles that Jim was always talking about. My problem was, I wasn't good in arithmetic. I wondered if Peaches was good in arithmetic. I mean, you can never tell, right?

We won a game! At first I thought sure we were going to lose because Jim wasn't there and Marla had to coach us. But everything turned out okay. The Pumas got up first. They've got these cool-looking uniforms and they all act cool. They got six runs in the first inning and I thought it was all over. But then we got four runs. The next inning they got three runs, and we got three runs. The third inning they didn't get any runs and we didn't get any runs.

Okay, so who's up first in the fourth inning and gets on base? Me! I hit the ball to their shortstop and he threw it to first base, but it bounced off the first baseman's chest and I was safe. Then Brian gets up and hits a home run! It was the first great hit ever made by our team. And it tied the score.

We got all the way up to the end of the fifth inning with the score tied 11 to 11. There was only one more inning to go and we were going to get up last. Talk about nervous!

They scored only one run in the top of the sixth. It was

12 to 11, their favor. Their coach kept on saying that all they had to do was to keep us from scoring and they would win. Well, Joey DeLea gets up first and gets a walk. Then Frank hits a pop-up, but their shortstop drops the ball. You got two guys on base and up comes Mop. Marla gives her the sign to bunt.

"It's a bunt!" This big voice comes out of the stands. I turn and I see it's Rocky from the Eagles. Right next to him is Mr. Treaster. The guy's *always* hanging around.

Then the Pumas' coach calls time out and talks to his infield. I'm getting so nervous, I don't know what to do. I know Brian is up next, and since he can hit almost as good as me I think we got a chance even if Mop makes an out.

When we start to play again, their third baseman and their first baseman get real close in case Mop bunts. Mop sees them in close like that and looks at Marla. Marla gives the bunt sign again.

Their pitcher jerks around a lot when he throws the ball and you can hardly tell when he's going to let it go. He jerks around and pitches the ball. The first pitch almost hits Mop in the head. She gives that guy a look you wouldn't believe!

"It's a bunt!" Rocky's still yelling out from the stands.

The guy throws again and Mop hits a line drive right at him. He just gets out of the way and the ball goes into the outfield. Joey and Frank come in and the game is over. We win!

After the game everybody was slapping hands and giving each other high-fives and everything. Marla was smiling and she and Mop kind of ran toward each other and I thought they were going to hug or something. Then they stopped at the last minute and Mop gave Marla a high-five.

You know how it feels to win like that? It feels good! It feels so good, I was still smiling when I got home.

"How did the game go?" Dad asked.

"We won!"

"How did you do?"

"I won too," I said.

"Did you get any hits?"

"I got on base once," I said. "And I scored one run."

"Oh." It was the littlest *oh* you ever heard in your entire life.

"How'd the Moondance Kid do?" he asked Moondance.

"I got three hits but I missed one ball," Moondance said. "It bounced right off my glove."

"Hey, three hits, that's okay," Dad said. "All right!"

I didn't even remember Moondance getting three hits, but then I thought about it real hard and I remembered every time he got up. He got *four* hits. I told him that and he said one of them was an error. Marla told him that.

She didn't tell me anything. I guess because I didn't get any real hits.

I asked Mom if she could figure out why I didn't get any hits. She said she didn't know why and I told her about Jim's angles and how I wasn't too good at math. She said she didn't think that was the reason.

You know what I think? I read someplace where there are day people and night people. The day people do things better in the daytime, while the night people do things better at night. We play all our games in the day and I think I might be a night people.

Come to think of it, I'm pretty sure I'm a night people.

Mop missed the next game and we lost it. She was taking care of Taffy. She's the only one at the Academy who really knows how to take care of Taffy. I don't know how she knows how to take care of a baby llama, but she does. She said that the only thing wrong with Taffy was that she missed her mother. The new kid at the Academy, Artemis, said that Mop looked like a mama llama anyway. He thought that was pretty cool until Mop gave him a fat lip.

Jim was missing a lot of practices because of his job, but that was okay because Marla was a good coach. You didn't have to remember angles and things with her like you did with Jim.

When Marla found out that Mop was missing the game, she called up another girl, named Taisha, to take her place. Taisha came to practice, but she said she didn't like playing baseball that much.

"So how come you put your name down for the team?" Taisha lived down the street from me and I was walking her home.

"My uncle told my mother it would be good for me," she said.

"How come he said that if you don't like it?"

" 'Cause that's what he do," she said. "He gives people advice."

"That's his job?"

"Uh-uh," Taisha said. "That's just what he do, that's all."

"So you going to play?" I had to find out so I could tell Mop in case there was going to be trouble.

"If I don't, that guy, what's his name—Jim—said I could be a cheerleader."

"You going to do that?"

"Maybe," Taisha said. "People like cheerleaders a lot."

Two days later me and Mop were on the field sitting in the stands and I told her about Taisha.

"She cute?" Mop asked.

"She's okay," I said.

"And Jim said she could be a cheerleader?"

"That's what Taisha told me," I said. "She said she might be a cheerleader because everybody likes them."

"I ain't being no cheerleader. I don't care if everybody hates me," Mop said. She took a deep breath, deeper than maybe I had ever seen anybody take, and then let it out again.

"What's wrong?"

"Everything," she said. "I don't think I'm going to get adopted. I think I'm going to have to go out to Riverhead."

"You'll get adopted," I said. "And even if you do have to go out to Riverhead, you'll be okay."

"No, I won't," she said. "Here I am trying to be the best ball player around and soon's I miss a game they get somebody to take my place. They'd better get their act together pretty quick."

Mop started for the Academy and I sat in the stands. When you know somebody a long time, like me and Mop knew each other, you hate to see them sad because you know just how sad feels for them.

So she's sad and I'm sad. I'm thinking about what's going to happen to her, and if we're going to be friends if she has to move to Riverhead. Then somebody sits next to me and I look up and it's Mr. Treaster and on the other side of him is Rocky.

"So how you doing?" he asked.

"All right," I said. I really didn't want to talk to him.

"How's that team of yours doing?"

"We won a game," I said.

"I heard, I heard," he said. "Congratulations!"

He reached out and shook my hand.

"Thanks."

"This is a good league," Mr. Treaster said. "Lot of good young ball players in it."

"I guess so."

"You hear about that new kid on the Colts?"

"No."

"He played for Bayonne last year," Rocky said. "Hit about four-fifty, with twenty home runs."

"Nobody hits twenty home runs," I said.

"This kid did. He could probably ruin the Elks all by himself," Mr. Treaster said.

"He really hit twenty home runs?"

"It was in all the papers in Bayonne," Rocky said.

"You think the Colts might even win first place?" I asked.

"Beat us?" Mr. Treaster laughed. "No way!"

"I just wondered."

I watched as Peaches shuffled along the gate toward

the entrance to the ball field. He came through the gate and looked around, as if he was searching for something.

"It's a shame they don't lock the gates to keep people like that out of the park," Mr. Treaster said.

"I thought he was one of the Elks." Rocky picked up a stone and threw it toward the outfield.

"Say, you know what I thought would be one heck of a joke," Mr. Treaster said. "We should steal all of the Colts' signs and every time we played them we'd use the same signs as they did."

"Then they would know what you were going to do," I said.

"Sure, but that way it would all be equal," Mr. Treaster said. "They'd know our signs and we'd know theirs. What do you think, Rocky?"

"Yeah, that'd be fun," Rocky said.

"Hey, what are those letters they call you by?"

"T.J."

"You ever go to the Colts' practice, T.J.?"

"Sometimes. Sometimes they practice just before we do."

"You ought to get their signs and write them down, you know."

"I don't think that's right," I said.

"He's chicken," Rocky said.

"He's just nervous," Mr. Treaster said.

"Don't you guys know that baseball is supposed to be fun?" Mr. Treaster asked.

"We have fun," I said. I got up and jumped down into the field.

"Hey, R.J., where you going?" Mr. Treaster called after me.

"T.J.," I called back. "Not R.J."

"Well, where you running off to, T.J.?"

"Gotta go home," I said.

"Yeah, that figures," Rocky called.

I got near the gate and Peaches was leaning on it. He smelled bad. He looked at me and I looked at him and our eyes met for a while. Then he turned away and looked over toward the outfield. I turned away and went through the gate.

I liked Peaches. Maybe not a lot, the way you liked a friend, more like somebody you just knew a lot about. I felt that way about the kids at the Academy too. I liked them even if I didn't know them too well. In a way Peaches was like the kids in the Academy.

Marla called the next Wednesday to say that the practice had been canceled.

"You hear about the new kid on the Colts?" I asked her.

"Yes, I did. He's supposed to be pretty good," Marla said. "But what it really means is that the teams will be more balanced. That's going to give us a better chance."

Moondance and I went to the ballpark but there was a Pee-Wee game going on so we went over near the playground.

"What do you want to practice?" I asked.

"Let's practice catching," Moondance said.

That was cool with me. We both made believe we were outfielders and began throwing the ball to each other. Only thing was, Moondance could throw the ball farther than I could. I could stand near the fire hydrant, the one with the top painted yellow, and throw the ball almost to where the statue was. The statue was a soldier who had been in some war, only somebody had broken his gun off.

I threw the ball to Moondance and he missed it. He missed it by maybe fifteen feet. I figured he really needed the practice more than me. Then he threw it. Right over my head. He threw it from the statue all the way past the fire hydrant to a park bench.

I wasn't mad or anything, but Moondance is a lot smaller than me and he threw the ball farther. So I wound up and threw it with all my might. It went from the fire hydrant almost past the soldier. Moondance missed it again, but not by much this time.

"Hold it for a minute!" I called to him.

He held the ball and I watched the trees to make sure the wind wasn't blowing. I saw that in a karate movie once. This guy watched the trees to see if the wind was blowing and then as soon as the wind stopped he shot an arrow right through a keyhole and into the heart of the bad guy.

When I was sure the wind wasn't blowing to help him, I told him to throw. He threw it past the bench!

Okay, so we switched positions. I threw it from the statue. It almost reached the bench. Then he threw it way past me.

He could just throw the ball farther than I could. That was it. I couldn't figure out how he could do that, but he could.

There's a road right through the park, and who comes driving along it but Sister Carmelita. Mop is with her.

Moondance and me went over to the car.

"You guys want to come with me or you want to stay in the park?" Sister Carmelita asked.

"We'll stay in the park," Mop answered for us, sliding out of the car. "Unless you need us."

"I know these streets pretty well," Sister Carmelita said. "I grew up on Gifford, just five blocks from here."

We watched Sister Carmelita drive away.

"She's going around the neighborhood seeing how the parish can help the needy," Mop said. "What are you guys doing?"

"Catching," I said. "You know Moondance can throw farther than me?"

"That's cause he's lopsided," Mop said. "Put your feet close together, hold both your arms out, and close your eyes."

"Do what?"

"Hold both your arms out," she said, lifting my arms. "And close your eyes."

I did it.

"Why's he doing that?" I could hear Moondance ask.

"Yeah, how come I'm doing this?"

"Don't say anything," Mop said. "Just tell me how you feel."

"Stupid," I said.

"Yeah, but what else?"

"That's it. Stupid."

"See?" she said.

I opened my eyes. "See what?"

"You're pretty much balanced, right?"

"Yeah."

"Now watch when Moondance tries to do it."

Moondance closed his eyes, put his feet together, and held his arms out.

"How do you feel?" Mop asked him.

"Okay."

"You feel like you might fall over a little?"

"No."

"Not even a little?"

"Maybe a little," Moondance said.

"See?" Mop said.

"See what?" I asked.

"Moondance is a little lopsided," Mop said. "So he's got more weight on one side than he's got on the other. That's why he can throw a ball farther than you can, because he's got more weight on that one side. It's all relative."

"You think so?"

"Yeah, only some people are lopsided but all dogs are lopsided. That's why God gave them tails to balance themselves. You see a dog that acts like he's a little shaky and one thing you notice is that his tail is going back and forth. That's so he can balance himself."

"I don't believe that," I said.

"You don't have to," Mop said. "But it's true."

Later, we walked toward the Academy and Mop and I talked while Moondance mostly made believe he was an airplane. I told Mop about Mr. Treaster asking me to get the Colts' signals.

"You think it was a joke?" I asked.

"He probably wants to cheat," Mop said.

"That's what I figured too."

"You know what Marla said?" Mop stopped and looked right at me.

"What?"

"I told her I had heard about Taisha being a cheer-leader and all and I didn't want to be no cheerleader. Then I told her I wanted to catch and you know what she said? She said that I was going to catch the next game," Mop said. "She said that if I wanted to catch, I could catch."

"Okay with me."

"If Brian says anything, I'm going punch his lights out," Mop said. "And you gotta watch my back, okay?"

"Sure."

When I got home, I asked Dad if some people had more weight on one side of their body than on the other. He went into a long thing about how everybody was different and how some people might have slightly more weight on one side of the body than on the other. Then I told Moondance he needed a tail. You know what? He liked the idea.

I'm not sure what I want to be when I grow up. Sometimes I think I want to be a baseball player, or maybe a basketball player. But those aren't the kinds of things you can say to grown-ups. You have to say you want to be a doctor, or a lawyer, or a guy who sells insurance. It really doesn't matter what you really want to be, it's what you say you want to be that counts. Parents especially like you saying that you want to be something important. Even if you say you want to be something like the President of the United States, it's okay. As a matter of fact, that's probably a really cool thing to say.

Sometimes I think I want to be a scientist. I like science in school for one thing, and for another I like to do experiments. There's this one experiment I had been working on for a while with Moondance. It's where you put your hands together with the lights on, turn the lights out, and then open your hand to see if you captured any light. Moondance and I tried it four times and it never worked. But one day, when Moondance had gone to the library to get a book on lizards, I figured out a way it might work.

I took a Pepsi-Cola bottle and covered it with black paper and then covered the black paper with tape. I covered the whole thing except for the opening on top. Then I put the opening right in front of the light bulb on my lamp.

The way I figured it, the whole inside of the bottle was filled with light. Then I covered it with the top as quickly as I could and fastened it down tight. After I got that done, I turned the lights off in the room and shut the door so that it was really black. Then I couldn't find the bottle.

I turned the lights back on, found the bottle, and put it on my bed. Then I turned the lights back off. I found the bottle in the dark and put my eye right near the opening. Then slowly, slowly, I undid the bottle top. I kept my eye right there so if any light came out it would have to hit my eye.

Nothing.

I turned the lights back on and tried to figure out what went wrong. I had just about figured it out—that the time I took looking for the bottle had caused the light to fade away—when I heard this little yelp from Mom. It sounded like when you accidentally step on a dog's tail or something. I came running out of the room and Dad, who was in the living room, was right behind me.

"What happened?" Dad asked.

"I got beat up!" Moondance said.

He didn't have to say it, you could see it. His clothes were all messed up and dirty and he was crying.

"Oh, no!" Mom had her hand over her mouth.

"Where did it happen?" Dad asked.

"On the way from the library," Moondance said.

He was still carrying a library book and I could see that his hands were scraped and raw-looking.

"Did they take your money?" Mom asked.

"No, he just started up with me and then started pushing me," Moondance said. He was sniffling.

"Do you know the kid who did it?" Dad asked.

"Rocky," Moondance said, looking at me. "From the Eagles."

"How big is this kid?" Dad asked.

"Do you know this Rocky's last name?" Mom asked. "I'm calling his parents right now!"

"Just a moment." Dad held one hand up. "How big is this kid?"

"He's about this tall," Moondance said, holding his hand about three inches over his head.

"I see," Dad said. "Don't worry about it. Your brother will take care of it."

Dad turned and started back toward the living room. Mom went after him and I could hear her saying that she should call Rocky's parents. Dad was saying no, that boys got into fights and that was part of growing up.

I put my arm around Moondance's shoulders and took him into our room, praying Mom would win the argument.

Moondance wiped his face off with a T-shirt and managed a smile. In the other room I could hear Mom and Dad talking. She was still upset but he was calm. I could hear her saying that she didn't want us fighting. I couldn't hear what Dad was saying, but whatever it was it didn't do much to calm Mom down. After a while I heard her walk past our room, and then she came back and opened the door. Her face was a little puffy too. She had been crying.

She had a washcloth and wiped off Moondance's face. He was pretty much okay by that time.

"Your father says that T.J. will fight this boy," Mom said. "And that's the way it's going to be settled. He says I'm not to make sissies out of you."

She looked at me and her mouth tightened up. Then she put her hand on my shoulder and went out of the room. Then, a bit later, Dad knocked on the door.

"What was the fight about?" he asked Moondance.

"Nothing," Moondance said. "He just started up, that's all."

"T.J., I guess you can take care of this bully?" he said.

"Yeah," I said.

He winked at me and closed the door.

Mom and Dad didn't say a word during dinner. Not a word. After dinner Moondance and me watched television in our room before going to bed. He didn't say anything about the fight until after Mom had come in and kissed us and put the lights off.

"Hey, T.J."

"Yeah?"

"You know, I feel kind of bad about the fight," he said.

"He's bigger than you are," I said. "He's always picking on people."

"Not that," he said.

"What?"

"You know what started the fight?"

"How could I? I wasn't there."

"He said he heard we were adopted."

"Yeah?"

"And then he said my real parents must have really been ugly to have kids like you and me."

"What's he talking about? He looks like a pimple with ears."

"I hit him first."

"You did?"

"Yeah, then he really lit into me."

I tried to picture Rocky fighting Moondance. No matter how you look at it, Rocky was too big to fight Moondance.

"You hurt real bad?" I asked him.

"No, but you know why I feel bad?"

"Why?"

"Because I hit him because of what he said about our real parents," Moondance said. "That's why I didn't tell Dad. You think that was okay? To fight over our real parents?"

"Sure, you should have hit him."

"You think so?"

"Yeah."

"You really gonna fight him?"

"Sure."

"T.J., you want to know something about fighting Rocky?"

"What?"

"He's going to beat the daylights out of you."

"Oh."

That wasn't the best thing to hear in the whole world, that was for sure.

Dad's mom goes to a Baptist church called Bethel Tabernacle. She told me that *Bethel* means "House of God," and *Tabernacle* means "tent." Only it's a brick church and not a tent.

Grandma Lois is really round, but she don't seem fat. She's got dark skin, like Dad's, and her eyes are like his, but not exactly. I'm not sure if it's because she has ladies' eyes or because they're just a little different.

Dad's a Baptist and Mom is Catholic, but she helps out in Grandma's church sometimes. The church was giving a recital and she was helping to decorate the room it was being held in. Mop was over to our house the next day after practice and didn't want to go back to the Academy so Mom called Sister Carmelita to see if she could go to Bethel with us and Sister Carmelita said it would be okay.

"And who are you, little lady?" Grandma Lois wiped her hands off on a towel and lifted Mop's chin up so she could see her better.

"Mop."

"Mop?" Grandma Lois turned her head and looked down at Mop like she didn't believe her. "Now what kind of people be naming their child some Mop?"

"That ain't my real name," Mop said. "My real name is Olivia Parrish but everybody calls me Mop on account of the initials of Miss Olivia Parrish is *M-O-P*, which is Mop."

"And you like them calling you that?"

"It's better than some dumb old Olivia!" Mop said.

"And you T.J. and you the Moondance Kid, right?" Grandma Lois was starting her laugh.

When Grandma Lois laughed, it didn't just come out

◆ 73

of her mouth the way some people's laugh comes. It started way down in her stomach and you could see it shaking. Then she would start to rock like she was getting ready and you could see the laugh coming and then when it got up to her head her whole face would light up and the laugh would come out and fill up the room so good, it would make you laugh too.

"Lord, if you kids ain't a mess, ain't *nothing* a mess!" She started laughing and we were all laughing.

Even Mom laughed, which was good because she had been sad ever since Moondance and Rocky got into the fight.

"Do you mind if they stay up here and read or something until we're finished downstairs?" Mom asked.

"No, they can do what they want," Grandma Lois said. "Let me see if there's any soda or anything in here."

We were in the church kitchen and Grandma Lois looked in the refrigerator for soda. There wasn't any soda, but she found some lemonade. She poured three glasses and put them on the table.

"We don't have any cookies or anything like that . . ." she said.

"We can make some cookies," Mop said. "If you got the stuff."

"I don't think the church needs you to make a mess up here while we're cleaning up downstairs," Mom said.

"Girl, let them mess around a little if they want. Foots used to love to make cookies when he was little."

"Who's Foots?" I asked.

"Foots? That was what we used to call your daddy," Grandma Lois said. "First we started calling him Foot-to-foot. That's 'cause every step I would make he'd be right behind me, holding on to my house dress. If he couldn't see me, he'd be yelling out all over the place. 'Mama! Mama!' "

"Dad used to do that?" Moondance asked.

"Didn't he? And if he walked outside the door and he lost sight of me for two minutes, he'd be screaming bloody murder. He was the biggest little mama's boy you ever wanted to see, and I loved every minute of it!"

Grandma Lois threw her head back and laughed and everybody else laughed too.

"So we might as well make some cookies," Mop said.

"You really know how to make cookies?" I asked.

"Sure, all we need is some flour and stuff," she said, looking up in the closet over the sink. "I'll be the chef and tell you guys what to do."

"How come you have to tell us what to do?"

"You know how to make cookies?"

"No."

"See?"

Mop couldn't find the regular flour so she used instant biscuit mix, which she said was just about the same thing. The first thing we did was to put two cups of mix in a big bowl. Moondance started cleaning up what we spilled as Mop and I added some milk and started stirring it up.

"You hear about Moondance and Rocky having a fight?" I asked.

"Yeah," Mop put a small pan on the stove and placed some butter in it. "So what are you going to do about it?"

"My mom thinks we should call his mother and tell her," I said. "But my dad thinks I should fight him."

"I think you should fight him too," Mop said.

"Yeah, but if he fights him, Rocky's going to beat him up," Moondance said.

"You got to sneak him," Mop said, "Walk up to him when he's not thinking about anything and knock him out. That's what I would do."

"What are you cooking the butter for?" I asked.

"It goes in the cookies," she said. "First you walk up to him and say something like 'Hey, Rocky, did you know it rains purple in Iran?' "

"It does?"

"No, but when you say that he'll think about it for a second." The butter was just about melted and she poured it into the mix. "Then you bop him one and jump all over him. That's what I did once when a guy hit my little brother."

"You don't have a little brother."

"He really wasn't my little brother but I called him that," Mop said. "Pour some of those raisins in."

There was a box of raisins on the shelf and I tried to pour some in, but they were all stuck together and came out in a lump. Mop started stirring them around and it started to look pretty good.

"He was lucky, too," Mop said. "I used to take karate classes and I learned how to reach right in between a person's ribs and snatch their heart out."

"You never went to no karate school, Mop," I said. "I've known you almost my whole life and I know nobody from the Academy has gone to karate school."

"I didn't say karate *school*," she said. "I said Karate

classes, which I took off the TV when I watched Bruce Lee."

"I guess I'll have to fight Rocky," I said.

"Sure," Mop said. "Put some sugar in."

"How much?"

"How much they got?"

I found a small box that was about a quarter full. "Not much" I said.

"Put that in."

I dumped that in and Mop stirred it up. Then we found a couple of big flat pans and Mop started dropping the dough on them in big lumps. In fact, we all did that. Then we put them in the oven.

We talked about a few other things, mostly about how the Academy was fixing to close. Then we started talking about the llama.

"Mostly I'm worried about Taffy," she said. "You know she's too big to just send back to California and she's too big for people to want her just because she's cute and everything. You know what I mean?"

"I think somebody will take Taffy," I said.

"I don't know," Mop kind of mumbled to herself. "I don't see anybody in too big a hurry."

Then we talked about the old days at the Academy. It was funny in a way. When me and Moondance were at the Academy, all we talked about were the days coming up and being adopted. But since I had left the Academy I could look back on it and think it wasn't so bad.

"Even if Taffy gets to go to a zoo far away it won't be so bad," I said. "She'll probably be happy in any zoo she goes to."

"I don't think so," Mop said.

"Mop, you going to cry?"

"I think so."

She cried a little, softly, the way she does when she's real unhappy. I didn't say anything. One thing we agreed on a long time ago in the Academy. When somebody was sad, you could be near them and everything, but mostly you just let them be. That's because most of us couldn't do anything to stop their being sad. It helped having somebody near, though, and I went and sat next to Mop and put my arm around her.

"The cookies are going to be good," I said.

"I think they're going to be more like cupcakes," Mop said.

"They'll still be good."

"T.J., how come I can't talk to Marla?" Mop shook her head. "Every time she gets near me I get so mumble-mouthed she must think something's wrong with me."

"Maybe because you're doing two things with her," I said. "You're playing ball for her and you're waiting around to see if she and her husband are going to adopt you."

"You remember how Sister Marianne talked about teamwork and all that?"

"Uh-uh."

"Yes, you do. Remember she was talking about the game of life and all that stuff?"

"Oh, yeah."

"I think that's what Marla's thinking about. If I can play ball all right, I can play the game of life."

"If that's what she's thinking, then it's not fair."

"Maybe, but it might be the only chance I got."

We heard somebody coming and Mop wiped her face with her hands and squeezed out a smile. It wasn't what you would call a great smile. In fact, it looked a little like she had a cramp or something. Then we took the cookies out of the oven.

Actually, they were more like cupcakes, but they were pure, one hundred percent delicious! They were the best cookies I have ever had in my entire life. We had made twelve altogether and we gave two to Moondance, one to Grandma Lois, one to Mom, and then me and Mop split the rest. She was taking some back to the Academy and I was going to take the rest home. That turned out to be three because Mop and me had both eaten one.

We played the Lions Thursday afternoon. Mike was supposed to pitch, but he hurt his thumb so Moondance pitched. Mop caught and we beat the Lions easy. Everybody was talking about how good Moondance pitched. Everybody except Evans, who always says you stink no matter what you do.

I didn't get any hits but I didn't make any errors either. Not what you would call real errors. A girl on the Lions tried to steal third base and Mop threw me the ball. I didn't catch it, but I knocked it down and Jim said it was a good play.

I didn't get any hits because I was nervous on account of Rocky. He was hanging around watching the game. I was standing near the fence talking to Mop when he came up on the other side of the fence.

"Your brother tell you I knocked him down?"

"He told him and you'd better not be around after the game," Mop said.

"Oh, yeah?" Rocky spit between his teeth right through the fence and on my sneaker. "What's going to happen if I'm around after the game?"

"T.J.'s going to wipe your face in the dirt which you

probably won't even mind since you're a maggot anyway!"

"I'll be around after the game," Rocky said. "And I'm going to hit you so hard I'm going to knock one of your initials right off your name, punk."

"Where you gonna be, Monkey Breath?" Mop banged her bat against the fence in front of Rocky. "Under the stands swallowing some more of your ugly pills?"

I had to get up. I struck out on three pitches and I could hear Rocky laughing. That's okay, we still won.

After the game everybody left except me, Moondance, Mop, Evans, and Rocky. Mop told Evans that Rocky had hit Moondance and that I was going to punch Rocky's lights out and Evans went and got Rocky and brought him over.

"He said he gonna punch your lights out!" Evans said in his real high voice. "That's what happens when you be messing with people's brothers."

You notice all this time I didn't say anything? You wonder why I didn't say anything? Because I was scared, that's why.

"Go on, knock him out!" Mop said.

I put my hands up and Rocky punched me in the face. In the nose. It felt like my whole face was on fire. It hurt something terrible!

"Now he really mad!" I heard Evans say.

Wham! Rocky punched me again, this time on the arm.

"Hit him back!" Mop was yelling.

Wham! Rocky jumped on top of me and I went down. He sat on me and put his knees on my arms so I couldn't move.

"Say 'I'm a stupid dog' or I'll knock your teeth out!" Rocky looked like a giant.

I tried to twist away from him but he hit me in the face again. Then he got up and told me to get up if I wanted some more.

I didn't want any more so I didn't get up. Rocky laughed and spit on the ground right near me. Then he walked away.

"Your nose is bleeding," Mop said.

I got up and started brushing myself off. I looked over at Moondance and he was crying. Rocky was still standing near the fence. I was really mad.

I went over to him and he stepped away from the fence. I pushed him back into it and then he hit me in the nose again.

This time I fell down hard and grabbed my nose because I thought it was broken. I heard Mop yelling at Rocky and then felt somebody helping me up.

"That's two things you can't do," Evans said, holding two fingers up in front of my face. "You can't play baseball and you can't fight!"

Me and Moondance went with Mop back to the Academy and I washed up there. I didn't want Dad to know that I had gotten beat up by Rocky. You know, Evans didn't make a big deal of it, and neither did Mop, but I thought Dad would.

Moondance left for home but I didn't want to go. Not right away. I was sitting around talking with Mop and she was telling me what I should have done to Rocky. She made it sound easy.

We were sitting in the Academy's auditorium, which

was really a gym with a stage on one end of it. The door
opened and Sister Carmelita came in. Soon as I saw her I
knew she was in some kind of trouble.

"You remember how I buy food for needy families?"
she asked.

"Sure," I said. I had gone around with her before I left
the Academy, buying food in the supermarket and helping Sister Carmelita to give it out.

"Well, today I met this man—he said his name was Mr.
Brown—and he said I didn't know anything about what
poor people like to eat," Sister Carmelita said. "So I
think I know what poor people eat because I was poor all
my life. But still I'm thinking, maybe he's right."

"So then what happened?"

"So then he tells me to give him the money and he
would go into the A&P on the Boulevard and buy the
food. I should go get the station wagon to take the food
around in."

"And you did it?"

"I did it," Sister Carmelita said. "But when I got back
to the A&P he was gone. I knew he would be gone all the
way back from the Academy. I said to myself, 'Titi, he's
going to be gone.' "

"Titi?"

"I used to be Titi before I was Sister Carmelita," she
said.

"Did you call the police?" I asked.

"T.J., I don't want to call the police. I told Sister Marianne I just missed him, that I didn't lose the money. But I
don't feel right calling the police. I did something stupid,
and I want to make it up. But seventy dollars . . ."

She put her hands to her head.

"What are you going to do?" Mop asked.

"Maybe look for him," Sister Carmelita said. "I got one idea who might find him for us."

Mop and I decided to go along with her. I wasn't in that much of a hurry to get home anyway. Bergen Avenue was really tough, and if it had been dark, I might not have wanted to go over there. When we got to Bergen a couple of people gave us looks, but one of the guys on the corner recognized Sister Carmelita as a nun even though she didn't wear a habit or anything, so I thought we were okay. All the same, I was glad when the cracked wooden door we knocked on opened. But when I saw who opened the door, I was really surprised. It was Peaches.

Peaches didn't open the door all the way. He stood looking at Sister Carmelita as she told him what had happened.

"I thought maybe you might know him," Sister Carmelita said.

Peaches shrugged. "This guy knew you was a nun and he still pulled that dirty trick on you?" he asked.

"He knew it was money for the poor," Sister Carmelita said.

"What he say his name was?"

"Mr. Aaron Brown," Sister Carmelita answered.

"How he look?" Peaches asked.

"He's got a real big head," Sister Carmelita said. "And he's got a scar on his chin."

"Big-headed, mean-tempered fool with yeller teeth?" Peaches asked.

"That's him!" Sister Carmelita said.

"That ain't no Aaron Brown." Peaches shook his head. "That's Buster Greene. He's about the meanest man in this city. He'd steal the pennies offen a dead man's eyes and pass 'em to his own mama for nickels."

"He's not dangerous or anything, is he?"

"He a dangerous man," Peaches said. "Everybody know that Buster Greene would rather hurt you than say hello."

"Then maybe we'd just better forget the whole thing," Sister Carmelita said.

"You got another dollar?" The shirt Peaches was wearing had the collar ripped off and he looked funny when he buttoned it up to the top. "I think we might be able to do something about Mr. Buster Greene."

"Peaches, I have two dollars left," Sister Carmelita said. "You're not trying to take my last two dollars, are you?"

"Naw," Peaches said. "I just got me a idea how we can get Buster loose from that money. You ever hear tell about Four Times Seven?"

None of us had heard about any Four Times Seven and me and Mop wasn't sure about whether Peaches was being honest or whether he was just trying to get a dollar to buy some wine.

Peaches told Sister Carmelita to give him the dollar and go back to the Academy. He would do the rest.

"I'm going with you," I said.

"Come on along if you want," Peaches said.

"Me too," Mop said. Sister Carmelita said she was going to go back to the Academy to pray.

Peaches, me, and Mop went over to Fairview, where a

friend of his lived. It was an old woman who didn't have a shape. She had a shape, but not a shape where you could say she was shaped like this or shaped like that. She just sort of lumped out all over the place. She was sitting in her window and we talked to her from the sidewalk. Peaches started telling her what Buster Greene did.

"Miss Sally, guess what that Buster Greene done did?"

"Honey, that lowlife might have done some of anything!"

"Do tell!"

"What he done now?"

"He done robbed a nun!"

"He did?"

"Sure as I'm standing here!"

"You know the Lord don't like you messin' with His people!"

"Ain't that the truth!"

"Who these kids?"

"They the nun's friends," Peaches said. "We trying to figure out a way to get they money back."

"Peaches, you gonna do something to make a fool outta Buster, I just know you is!" Miss Sally shifted her weight from one big elbow to the other and leaned forward. "What you gonna do?"

"Well, I got me one dollar," Peaches said. "If you let me borrow some ketchup and Four Times Seven for about an hour, I'll see what I can do."

"Four Times Seven?" Miss Sally turned her head to one side and pursed her lips. "Peaches, you always been a figuring fool. I'll let you borrow him if you wait while I gets dressed so I can see what you gonna do."

I wanted to know what he was going to do too. We went across the street to a small store and Peaches bought a small can of shaving cream. By the time we got back to where Miss Sally lived, she was out on the sidewalk. She was wearing a dress that didn't have much color to it and house shoes that flapped when she walked. In one hand she carried a stick and in the other she had a bottle of ketchup. Next to her was a shopping cart and in the shopping cart was a box, the kind you keep animals in.

"How is he today?" Peaches asked, bending over so he could take a good look at the box.

"He okay," Miss Sally said. "He ain't been fed yet though."

"That in there is Four Times Seven," Peaches said.

Two guys came down the street and stopped and looked at the box.

"He in there, Miss Sally?" a light-skinned guy asked.

"He in there," Miss Sally said.

They looked at the box from a little distance. I looked at Mop and Mop was leaning over trying to see what was in the box. We heard a growl come from the box and we all backed off.

"Four Times Seven was born with seven toes on each foot," Peaches said. "That's how he got his name. He's the meanest cat that ever walked the face of the earth."

"A cat?" Mop asked.

"He ain't just no cat," Miss Sally said. "That's Fo' Times Seven!"

"When he was nothing but a kitten he chased a dog

through the streets of Baltimore until the dog dropped dead from a heart attack!" Peaches went on.

"Tell 'em about that rattlesnake he killed in Monroe, Louisiana," Miss Sally said. "A mojo man tried to throw a rattlesnake on me, and Fo' Times Seven grabbed it and shook it till every one of its rattles come off and it had to shed its skin to get away."

"He a legend in his own time," Peaches said. "Just like Babe Ruth or Joe Louis. A hobo in East St. Louis tried to kill him by throwing him in the water. But he just swum to shore nice as you please. That hobo tried to throw him in a fire, but he just come out with half his fur burned off and a grin on his face."

"He got hit by a taxi once, and that didn't kill him," another guy said. "And I seen that with my own eyes and I knowed the Egyptian fella what was driving the cab!"

Miss Sally started pushing the shopping cart down the street. Peaches went after her. Some people were looking at us, but I was listening to the growls coming from the box!

We started down the street to where Peaches said Buster lived. Peaches was leading us and Miss Sally was right behind him pushing the shopping cart that held the box Four Times Seven was in.

"Yo! Peaches, what y'all doing, man?" a guy called out as we passed a Bar-B-Que joint.

"They gonna take care of Buster!" Miss Sally called out.

"Buster *Greene*?"

"That's right!" Peaches called back.

When Peaches said that it was Buster Greene we were

going to take care of, everybody started following us. They weren't the coolest-looking people in the world, either. A tall, skinny man ran up to Peaches and started telling him how he had better leave Buster alone.

"Buster the meanest man in the world!" The tall, skinny guy had a patch over one eye. He reached up and switched the patch to the other eye, which seemed just as good as the first.

"He done robbed a nun," Peaches said. "It's high time somebody took care of him."

"Hey, Peaches, you really got Four Times Seven in there?"

"It ain't no Ting Ling panda bear," Peaches said.

Buster lived in a house that leaned to one side. There was a barber shop one flight up with a barber pole painted on a stick outside of it. The barber came out with a comb and a pair of scissors in his hand.

"What's going on?" he called down the stairs.

"Peaches is gonna mess up Buster Greene!" the skinny man with the patch over his eye called up.

"Peaches." The barber was a fat man with heavy jowls that hung down the side of his face. "You better get on out of here before Buster tear your butt up!"

"Peaches got Four Times Seven with him!" an old woman called out.

"They ain't no Four Times Seven," the barber said. "That's just a old wives' tale."

"Then why don't you come on down and mess with what's in this box!" Peaches said.

The barber came down a few steps and looked at the box in the shopping cart. Then he tilted his head to one side and looked again. "Even if there is a Four Times Seven, he can't do nothing with no Buster Greene!" the barber said.

As Peaches went up to the front door of Buster Greene's house, I could have sworn I saw something move away from the open window. Peaches banged on the door.

"Buster! I got to have a word with you!"

There was a stirring in the folks who had moved around us and Miss Sally told them all to hush up.

The door to Buster's house opened up and he stood there, brown and bald-headed and looking as mean as he wanted to look.

"What you want?" he asked. He looked over Peaches' shoulder at the crowd. The whole crowd moved back a little.

"You done took some money from a nun," Peaches said. "And I come to get it back."

"I don't know what you talking about," Buster said. Actually he didn't say it so much as he just growled it out. "And you better get on out my face before I lose my temper!"

The crowd stepped back again.

"I'm serious, Buster!" Peaches stepped back until he reached the shopping cart with Four Times Seven in it.

"I said *git*!" Buster opened the door a little wider.

People started leaving right away and I felt like going myself. In a minute I looked around and the only ones there were me, Mop, Peaches, Miss Sally, and Buster standing in the doorway looking like King Kong's ugly cousin. Everybody else had backed off and were looking from across the street.

If I had been a little less scared, and my feet a little less heavy, I would have run too. But if I had, I would have missed seeing Four Times Seven in person.

Peaches took the box out of the cart and put it in front of Buster. Buster looked down at it and reached for something behind the door. There was a cord hanging out of the box and Peaches grabbed on to it and wrapped it around his wrist. When the box opened, Four Times Seven came out.

Four Times Seven looked like a cat, but he was as big as a dog. There was as much of him missing as there was there. Part of one ear and half his tail were gone, and there were chunks of fur missing from all over his body. Some of the fur that was left was black and the rest of it was a dirty gray. He hissed and strained on the leash until Miss Sally went over and pointed at Buster.

"Sic 'em! Sic 'em!"

Four Times Seven lunged forward until it reached the end of the leash. Then it stood up on its back legs and tried to claw at Buster. I moved around to where I could get a good look. What I saw was the ugliest cat I had ever seen in my whole life. Its head was at least as big around as a dinner plate. One eye looked one way and the other one looked in a different direction altogether. Spit was coming from its mouth, but I couldn't see any teeth. Its gums were red and its black lips were curled back.

Buster took one look and slammed his door shut. Peaches bent down, picked up Four Times Seven, and pitched him through Buster's open window. The moment the cat was in, Peaches slammed the window shut.

I never heard so much hollering and banging around. Peaches was pulling on the knob of Buster's door so Buster couldn't get out.

The skinny man with the patch over his eye had come back. He saw what had happened and came over, and he and Miss Sally held the window down. Buster's face appeared at the window and I could see he was scared stiff. His eyes were rolling around and his whole face was straining as he tried to lift the window. Then I saw a black and gray blur leap up on his shoulder and attack his face. It was Four Times Seven!

It took Buster two more times trying to get out the door and one more time trying to get out the window before an envelope came out from under the door.

"Count it!" Peaches shouted.

Miss Sally got the envelope and threw it to Mop. Mop started counting the money.

"Sixty-eight dollars and two cents!" Mop said.

"That's close enough," Peaches called out. "Get the box ready!"

Miss Sally moved away from the window and opened the box. Then Peaches moved away from the door. We heard something bang hard against the window, then we heard a yell, and then the door flew open. Buster came running out with his face covered with scratches.

"Man, did you see how he was messed up?" somebody called out.

I was starting to look into Buster's house when something hit me and knocked me backward! For a moment

my eyes were closed. When I opened them, I was looking up into the face of Four Times Seven.

"I got him!" I could hear Peaches' voice.

I heard his voice, but I couldn't move. Four Times Seven was on my chest and I could feel his warm breath in my face. He opened his mouth wide and I thought my heart would stop. He didn't have a tooth in his mouth, but that didn't stop him from clamping down on my face!

Everything went black and I died. Or maybe I nearly died, because I know my heart wasn't beating when Four Times Seven clamped down on me like that. When his mouth came off my face, it came off with a sucking sound that pulled my head right off the ground.

"Get him up before he gum that boy to death!" I think I could hear Mop's voice. They were trying to pull Four Times Seven off me. They had him but he had me. His claws were dug into my shirt.

Finally, Peaches put his foot on my chest and pulled the animal away from me. Part of my shirt went with him.

Funny, I saw them push him back into the box and fasten it up, but I couldn't move the whole time they were doing it. When Mop got to me and asked me if I was okay, I didn't know what to say. Peaches was looking at my shirt at where Four Times Seven had pulled big pieces of it away.

"Boy, you okay," he said. "He didn't get no flesh."

They helped me up and the crowd that had gathered around started cheering.

"Four Times Seven must be getting old," Miss Sally said. " 'Cause when he was young he'd a killed you stone dead!"

I thanked her for sharing that with me.

Peaches went with me and Mop to the Academy to take the money back to Sister Carmelita. Sister Marianne was there and she was really glad that we got the money back, but all the time we were telling how we got it back she was crossing herself. She was even smiling, so I guessed she didn't think it was so bad.

"Mr. Peaches, would you like a job?" Sister Marianne asked when we were finished.

Peaches looked at me and shrugged his shoulders. "I got to tell you the truth," he said. "I don't know what I can do that's worth anything."

"You can help us to find out the needs of the poor in the neighborhood," Sister Marianne said. "And I'm sure there'll be a lot of things to be done around the church, even after the Academy has closed."

"If that's what you want," Peaches said, "well, that's just okay with me."

Mop's mouth kind of twisted funny when Sister Marianne mentioned the Academy's closing. Nobody noticed much except me, I think. Sister Marianne and Sister Carmelita were both glad to be doing something for Peaches, and I think that Peaches was glad to be getting a job.

Peaches walked me home.

"Say, Peaches, what happened to Four Times Seven's teeth?" I asked.

"He ain't never had no teeth as long as I've known about him," Peaches said. "Some say that before Miss Sally got him, he was owned by an old-time blues player in East St. Louis. A fellow broke into the little railroad flat where the blues player lived and robbed and killed him. They say that Four Times Seven trailed the man that killed his master all the way to Hot Springs, Arkansas, and lost all his teeth chewing through a concrete wall to get at him."

"He got him?" I asked.

"That's what they say," Peaches said.

"You think I could borrow him sometime?"

"What you want a mean cat like that for?"

"There's this guy . . ." I started to tell Peaches about Rocky, but then I changed my mind. "I guess I don't want to borrow him."

"T.J." Peaches stopped outside my door. "Some of us are like Four Times Seven, we a little like the animals. We good at fighting and scratching our way through life. Some of us ain't. Some of us is gentle and kind and worried about other people more than we worried about ourselves. They the best kind of people, boy. Don't let anybody tell you anything different, either. Me, I was always good at fighting and scratching. It ain't done me a whole lot of good, is it?"

"You're okay," I said.

"Yeah, I guess I am." Peaches had a big grin on his face. "I sure had me a good day today!"

"So did I," I said. "So did I."

t's official. Marla is now head coach of the Elks. Mr. Kennedy had to leave for two weeks to do some kind of aerospace work in California and he gave up the team to Marla. Everybody was sorry to see him go, but we weren't too sorry to see his angles go. We all liked Marla, anyway. Mr. Treaster came around to our practice and asked Marla if she wanted one of the men from the Elks Club to take over the team.

"No, sir." Marla smiled. "I think I can handle the team nicely, thank you."

Mr. Treaster didn't say anything, but he gave her that smile he does sometimes and you could see that he was thinking a lot.

"What we have," Marla was saying after Mr. Treaster left, "is a pretty good team. We've lost some games we could have won, but we're not that bad. What we need is a pitcher for the big games. Also, we have to make a lot fewer errors."

"Hope you're not going to make a whole bunch of stupid changes," Brian said.

"What makes you think I might?" Marla asked him.

"Mr. Treaster said so," Brian said. "He said that

you're probably going to try to make the girls the stars of the team or something."

"Is that so terrible?" Marla asked.

"It is," Brian said, "when they stink!"

Mop went after Brian and tackled him around the stomach. They went flying down to the ground and started rolling around the pitching mound.

"Punch her out!" Evans started hopping around them in a circle. "Punch her out!"

"Use your knuckles!" Chrissie was holding her fist up and tapping on her knuckles as if either Mop or Brian could see her.

They couldn't. They were still on the ground in a cloud of dust. Every once in a while you could see a fist come up and go back into the dust. They were both kicking, too.

Marla tried to stick her leg between theirs to pry them apart and a moment later she was on the ground too. Mop and Brian were swinging away and Marla was on top of them.

Some kids from the Pumas came over and asked us what was going on.

"It's a fight, stupid!" Evans said.

"Hey, don't call me stupid, stupid!" the guy said.

That's how the second fight started.

The third fight didn't start over anything, Joey DeLea just punched one of the kids who was standing watching the first two fights. Then everybody was fighting and then some cops came over and broke it all up.

"You kids are a disgrace to Little League baseball!" It was the coach of the Pumas. "Where's your coach?"

"There she is." Chrissie pointed to Marla, who was still sitting on Brian. Her face was red and covered with dust and her hair was matted down on her forehead.

"You're the coach of the Elks?" The Pumas' coach looked down at Marla. "And you're fighting with them?"

"No," Marla said, getting to her feet. "I'm teaching them how to slide, okay?"

"I can't see how you're teaching them how to slide like that," the Pumas' coach said. "That doesn't make a bit of sense."

But Marla had already started off the field, and the rest of the Elks were following her.

Marla did make some changes. Jim used to tell us not to swing unless the ball was right over the plate. He always said that a walk was just as good as a hit.

"A walk is just as good as a hit," Marla said, "but it's not nearly as much fun. I want everybody up there trying to get a hit."

Everybody started swinging like crazy, and some of us even started hitting like crazy. Brian hit two home runs our next game, Mike got four hits and almost five but a guy made a lucky catch on him. Mop was hitting like crazy.

Moondance was hitting pretty good too. I wasn't. Marla said I wasn't swinging level. You know what I think happened? Jim had told us so much about hitting at the right angle that I was swinging at an angle instead of level. That's why I was missing the ball.

"Are you looking at the ball at all?" Marla asked me when I struck out for the third time against the Hawks.

"Sure," I said.

"Maybe your bat's a little heavy," she said.

I hadn't thought of that. That would make two problems at one time. The first problem is that I couldn't swing at the right angle if the bat was too heavy, and the second was that maybe since I was using the same bat that I was using when Jim was the coach it kept reminding me of swinging at an angle.

I changed bats. I think the one I switched to might have been too light because I struck out again, but I struck out over the ball instead of under it. The way I figure it, sooner or later I'll get just the right bat and then *wham!* I'll probably be knocking them over the fence all the way to second base of the *next field*!

Anyway, we won three games in a row! Not only that but the Eagles lost another game. Everybody was talking about us meeting the Eagles in the play-offs. Taisha said she was going to get herself a regular cheerleading outfit.

"How can you have just one cheerleader?" Brian asked.

"Because only one guy gets up at a time, stupid," Taisha said.

"We're lucky to have even one cheerleader," Marla said, stepping in between them. "But what we really need is a strong pitcher. The Eagles do very well when they face a weak pitcher, but not that good against the good pitchers in the league."

Mike was a pitcher. Lo Vinh pitched sometimes, Brian pitched sometimes, and Moondance did too. Lo Vinh was real serious about the games. Whenever anyone made a mistake, he would start yelling at them in Vietnamese. Everybody hated that because nobody knew what he was talking about. He even talked to himself when he made a mistake.

But you know who threw the hardest? Moondance. He even threw harder than Brian, but he didn't throw the ball that straight.

So we won the three games and everybody is getting kind of happy with the team. Brian really wasn't too happy. He wanted everyone to be more serious about the game. Especially Chrissie. She keeps the same smile on her face no matter what happens.

"When you miss a ball you're not supposed to be smiling, dummy!" Brian yelled at Chrissie.

Chrissie looked at him and smiled.

We were supposed to play the Pumas for the last time that Saturday. If we beat them, we would have second place wrapped up for sure and then we would be in the play-offs. That's why we were having an extra practice.

Marla had Mike pitching to us. He could throw the ball over the plate better than anybody. She made Chrissie, who tried to bunt every time she got up (which also made Brian mad) practice her bunting.

You could tell Chrissie to swing away, but she never would. She would always bunt. Most of the time the other team would throw her out. But sometimes their third baseman would make an error and throw the ball wrong or the first baseman would miss it. Then Chrissie would get on base, take the bobby pins from her hair, put them in her mouth, and then fix her hair. Meanwhile everybody would be yelling at her to get ready in case the next guy, who was Moondance, got a hit or something. It never bothered her though. She would just smile that little smile and go on fixing her hair until she was ready.

I got up after Chrissie and Marla told me to practice bunting too. I didn't want to. I told Marla I didn't think I should practice bunting.

"You have to help the team any way you can, T.J.," she said. "And bunting might be the way you can help best."

I didn't do it. It made me feel a little bad to bunt. I'm not sure why. Maybe it was because the only other person on the team who bunted was Chrissie. I don't know. I just sat down. I didn't want to do that either because I knew everybody was looking at me. But I just did.

"If you don't practice," Marla said in a voice that sounded like a teacher's, "you don't play."

I stood at the plate. When Mike threw the ball I just moved the bat a little. I didn't really bunt at it. I did that twice and then Marla told me to go into the outfield. I could tell Marla was mad at me because I didn't bunt. But that was okay because she was just starting to be the real coach of the Elks and didn't know how good I could hit.

Saturday was the day of the Pumas' game and I was really excited. Dad asked three times when the game was going to start. I was in a good mood, but it didn't last too long. When me and Moondance got to the Academy to pick up Mop, we got some bad news about Taffy. The zoo didn't want her after all.

"What will they do with her?" Moondance asked.

Sister Carmelita shrugged. "Maybe we can find a farm that will take her," she said. "There are a lot of llama farms out west."

"Let's get to the game," Mop said. "We'll talk about Taffy later."

We had to play the Pumas, and then we had to play the Hawks. If we beat the Pumas, then we would have second place and be in the play-offs against the first-place team which we knew already was going to be the Eagles. If we lost to the Pumas, we could still get into the play-offs by beating the Hawks.

"We want to beat the Pumas," Marla said when we got to the field. "If we do, then we can relax a little bit for the last game before the play-offs."

"We're not going to win the play-offs against no Eagles," Evans said. "They too good."

"We have a chance in a short series," Marla said. "We just have to win two games out of the three."

"How we gonna win two games when we ain't never won once against them?" Evans said.

"We're better than we were when we first played them," Marla said. "And we'll prove it."

Mike pitched for us and the Pumas scored five runs in the first inning. I wasn't playing. Marla had Lo Vinh playing third base instead of me.

"Why aren't you playing third base?" Dad had shown up shortly after the game started. "That kid they have out there now doesn't look that good."

"I don't know," I said. "Maybe Marla just wants to let him play for a while."

Dad's jaw tightened a little. And then he went up into the stands to watch the game.

By the third inning the score was 15 to 3 and I knew we were going to lose. Dad was right about Lo Vinh not being too good at third base. But then he hurt his hand and Marla brought in Jennifer! You ever see Jennifer play? If the ball goes two feet away from her, she won't even go for it.

Brian got mad and threw his glove down and Marla told him if he did that again, he would come out of the game.

"Hey, Marla, you got a great squad there!" Joe Treaster had shown up and was leaning against the fence. "I hope they make the play-offs!"

"So do I," Marla said.

A guy came down to the field and said he thought

Marla should put Moondance on third base and put Jennifer in the outfield.

"You go back into the stands and I will run this team!" Marla said in this real loud voice.

"Tell him, baby!" Mr. Treaster yelled again.

In the fifth inning we scored two runs and everybody got happy again. Marla switched Brian from short to pitcher and put Mike on shortstop. We were still way behind though.

In the top of the sixth Brian struck out the first Puma and Mop made a diving catch of a pop foul for the second out. The next two batters bunted balls down the third base line toward Jennifer. She didn't even try to run in for them. Brian got so mad he threw his glove at her. That's when Marla took him out of the game.

Brian's father was yelling at Marla. Mr. Treaster was yelling at her and laughing. I looked around to see what my Dad was doing and I saw him talking to Sister Carmelita.

"Hey! T.J.! Wake up!"

I turned and saw that Marla was pointing at me. I got my glove and went over to her.

She switched Mike back to pitcher, brought Joey DeLea in to play shortstop and put me in right field.

"Come on, guys," Marla said. "Let's prove we can stop them when we have to."

Mike loaded the bases by walking the next batter. Then their best hitter got up. He swung at the first pitch.

I could hear the crack of the bat and saw the ball coming right out to me. It looked like it was growing bigger as it came.

I went running in for it. I knew I was going to catch it. It came down and down. I was banging my glove with my fist. I was all ready to catch it.

It was a little higher than I thought.

I went back two steps and reached up as far as I could. The ball flew just over my glove. It bounced over the fence for an automatic double.

Everybody in the infield was throwing their gloves down and looking at me. Everybody.

Even from where I was standing, way in the outfield, all by myself, I could see Dad shaking his head. I knew what he was thinking. He was wondering how come he had such a lousy kid playing ball.

They scored one more run and then we got up. When I went in, I saw Marla talking to everybody. Then when I got to the bench they all said things like "Nice try" and "You almost had it." But nobody looked at me and I knew that Marla had told them to say that.

We didn't score that inning, but neither did the Pumas during the top of the sixth.

I got up in the last of the sixth. There were two outs and I missed the first two pitches. Then I bunted at the next ball and hit it but it went foul. Then the umpire called me out because of a rule about a foul bunt on the third strike being an out.

The Pumas won, 17 to 3.

After the game I didn't even want to go near Dad. He came over to where me and Jennifer were packing up the bases in the old blue duffel bag that we carried our stuff in and went up to Marla.

"Tough loss," he said.

"They're all tough losses, Mr. Williams," Marla said.

"Titi said that you might actually make the play-offs."
Dad shifted his weight from one foot to the other. "I
can't see how you're going to win."

I pushed home plate as hard as I could down to the
bottom of the bag.

"I don't know who this Titi is," Marla said. "But he
might have also told you that we scored some runs
against this team. If we had another pitcher besides
Brian, if Moondance could throw the ball over the plate,
for example, we would have a chance of at least being
respectable."

"Why don't you let Titi help?" Dad said. "She used to
be the best pitcher in our league."

"In the first place, I don't know this Titi," Marla said.
"And I think it's a little late with the play-offs starting
next week."

"You don't know Sister Carmelita?" Dad asked.

"Sister Carmelita?"

"Yeah, way back before she was a nun she used to play
Little League ball right here in Lincoln Park," Dad said.
"We used to call her Titi then. And she could *pitch*!"

Okay, so Sister Carmelita used to be a pitcher. But do
you know who really helped Moondance turn out to be a
good pitcher? Peaches! Okay, Peaches *and* Sister Carmelita.

Marla talked to Sister Carmelita and asked if she could
help Moondance. Sister Carmelita said that she didn't
know, but she would try. So we all went out to the playground the next day and Dad put the Sunday comics on

the ground for the plate. Moondance started pitching to
Mop.

Zip! Zip! Zip!

He could throw that ball over the plate so fast it wasn't
even funny.

Zip! Zip! Zip!

Marla shook her head.

"Let's see how you hold the ball, Moondance," Sister
Carmelita looked at how Moondance held the ball in his
hand.

"Like this," Moondance said, holding the ball up.

Sister Carmelita held his hand still and moved the ball
a little. "Try it that way," she said. "Don't let it touch
your palm. It's a little trickier, but I think you can do it."

The first ball that Moondance threw went right over
Mop's head.

"Follow through!" Sister Carmelita called out. "Bring
your arm all the way down."

Zip! Whack!

That's the way the ball went. It went even faster than it
did the first time he was throwing.

Zip! Whack!

The next ball went over Mop's head, but after that the
ball was going right into the glove.

Zip! Whack!

Zip! Whack!

"T.J., stand at the plate." Marla handed me a bat.

No way I wanted to stand there with the bat. I looked at
Marla to see if she really meant for me to stand there, but
she had already gone over to sit on one of the benches.
Dad was leaning against the backstop and Sister Car-

melita was standing near Moondance out at the mound. It was as if they were watching a show or something.

I looked at Moondance and he looked at me. He had his tongue out and was wiping off his pitching hand. Mop got down on her knees and put one hand behind her back.

"Throw it past him, Moondance!" she yelled. "He can't hit!"

"Don't swing, T.J.," Marla called out. "I just want to see his control."

Zip!

The ball went outside and against the backstop. Dad looked at Moondance and one eyebrow went up. Mop got the ball and threw it back to Moondance. Sister Carmelita was talking to him, but I couldn't hear what she was saying.

You know how I felt? A little nervous. Even though I didn't have to swing at the ball, you get a little nervous when Moondance throws it with all of his might.

Zip!

The ball went outside and past Mop's glove again.

"Give him a target, Mop!"

"I am giving him a target!" Mop yelled back as she picked the ball up again.

"C'mon, Son." Dad made a fist and held it up toward Moondance. "Bring it high and tight."

I didn't know what that meant, but I saw the next ball go flying outside again.

"Stand on the other side, T.J."

That's what Marla said.

"No!" That's what I said. Moondance was throwing the balls just where she wanted me to stand.

"You're not scared of the ball, are you?" Dad asked.

"No," I said.

I went to the other side. I wasn't scared of the ball. I mean, if the ball and me were in a dark room together, I wouldn't be nervous or anything. I was afraid of being *hit* by the ball.

Moondance wound up and threw the ball. I dropped the bat and got ready to duck in case it came toward me, but it didn't. It went on the other side.

"Moondance, are you afraid of hitting him?" Marla got off the bench and started toward us.

"I don't want to hit anybody," Moondance said.

"Don't worry about it, just throw the ball to Hop," Dad said.

"That's Mop, *M-O-P*." Mop gave Dad a look.

"If you just aim for Mop's glove, you won't be that close to him," Marla said. "You can almost do it with your eyes closed."

I got away from the plate. He wasn't throwing the ball at me with his eyes closed.

"Just keep your eye on the glove," Sister Carmelita said. "Take your time."

Moondance looked at Mop's glove and kept his eyes right on it. He wound up and threw the ball again.

Zip!

Fast as anything, but outside. I think they were right. He didn't want to hit me.

Then Dad caught and Mop got up to bat. Same thing. Moondance didn't want to throw the ball near anybody.

Dad said he would talk to him and I saw Moondance look a little sad. Sometimes Dad says things that sound good, or at least okay, but deep down you know they're not. He said he would talk to Moondance, that everything would be okay. But you could tell by the way he said it that he wasn't happy with the way Moondance pitched. I could tell it and Moondance could tell it too.

It's bad when you mess up and people aren't happy with you. Like when I missed the fly ball and everybody on the team threw their gloves down. But I think it's even worse when you do something good, like Moondance did, and somebody isn't happy with you because you didn't do it good enough. Especially when that somebody is your dad.

Still, Sister Carmelita had helped Moondance a little, and we didn't even know that Peaches was going to help too.

When we got home, Dad got out all these pictures of him playing baseball. He looked great. I imagined myself doing some of the things he did.

WILLIAMS'S HOMER SPURS ASU WIN!

"That's when we won the national championship," Dad said. "We made every paper in the state of Arizona every day that week!"

"That's where I first met him," Mom said. "All he ever talked about then was playing baseball. All he ever did was play baseball too. I think he married me because I could keep score."

Then he showed us the pictures of himself when he played for Kansas City.

"It must be hard to be a great baseball player," I said.

"Sometimes," Dad said. "It's even harder not to be a great ballplayer."

It wasn't even seven-thirty when Mom woke us up on Monday.

"We have a visitor!" she said. "Get dressed as quickly as you can!"

I got dressed first and started helping Moondance look for his sneakers.

"Mom seemed upset," I said.

"I heard Dad leave for work." Moondance was looking under the bed even though I had just looked for his sneakers there.

"Look in the closet."

"They're not there," he said.

"So where are they?"

"I don't know."

"Then how do you know they're not in the closet?"

"I just know."

I looked in the closet and found them. He smiled his stupid little smile and a moment later we went out to see who our visitor was.

"I want to ask you boys one question," Sister Marianne said. "And I want you to look me right in the eye and answer me truthfully."

"I'm sure the boys will answer you honestly," Mom said.

"Do either of you know where Taffy is?"

Sister Marianne looked at us one at a time.

Moondance said he didn't know, and I said I didn't know.

"How long has the llama been missing?" Mom asked.

"When I woke this morning some of the younger children at the Academy informed me that she was gone," Sister Marianne said. "I spoke to Sister Carmelita, who was all wide eyes and wonder but I was not—I repeat—not satisfied."

"Did you ask Mop?" Moondance asked.

"I asked Miss Olivia Parrish and she, too, was wide-eyed and full of wonder."

"Mop?" Moondance squinched up his nose.

"I didn't believe it either," Sister Marianne said. "The animal-protection people were to take the llama away today, and now it has mysteriously disappeared!"

"Would you care for coffee?" Mom asked Sister Marianne.

Sister Marianne said no, that she had to go to Newark on church business. "But I'll be back tomorrow evening and we'll get to the bottom of this, I assure all and sundry."

She left and we had to eat breakfast before going out to look for Mop. We had to know where Taffy was.

We found Mop at the Academy. She was oiling her glove. Not her catcher's mitt, which really belonged to the team, but her other glove. It was old, and beat up, and the strings were so messed up, you couldn't catch with it anyway.

"So I wake up and Taffy's gone," Mop says. She was chewing some grape bubble gum and you could smell it. "Sister Marianne told you that, right?"

"Right. You got any more bubble gum?"

"She tell you that Peaches is gone too?" She pulled a piece of bubble gum out of her pocket, broke it in half, and gave Moondance a piece and put the other piece into her mouth.

"He leave a note or something?"

"Uh-uh." Mop shook her head. "Nothing. You know what I think? I think he took Taffy and he's got her hid some place. You know what else I think?"

"What?"

"That if we don't find her soon, they're gonna make llama chops out of her."

"Get out of here," I said.

I knew she didn't mean that, because she didn't look really worried or anything.

We got ready for the game with the Hawks. We had to win to get into the play-offs.

At the field Marla was having everybody doing stretching exercises. Mop told her what had happened about Taffy.

I was a little worried. Because if they were going to let the animal-protection people take Taffy, that meant the Academy was just about ready to close. Also, Sister Marianne was going to Newark for something. Maybe that was about the Academy closing too. I didn't say anything to Mop, though.

Okay, the game started with us up first. We scored six runs in the first inning. Six runs. Brian was supposed to start the game, but after we scored six runs Marla told Frank to pitch. Frank's a really nice kid—he just looks mean. Also he gets really mad if you get a hit when he's pitching.

"Just let them hit the ball," Marla said. "Don't let them walk."

Their first two batters walked. But the next two struck out. The next guy tried to bunt and Mop threw him out at first. End of the first inning. Us 6, them zippo-rooni.

Second inning. We scored no runs and they scored one run. Score: us 6 and them 1.

Third inning. We scored nothing. They scored one. Score after three innings: us 6 and them 2.

Fourth inning. Joey struck out and Frank struck out. Then Mop hit a double and Brian hit a ball over the left-field fence. Everybody was going crazy jumping up and down. I looked over at the Hawks' bench and you know who was there talking to their coach? Mr. Treaster from the Eagles!

They didn't score anything. We were ahead 8 to 3.

Fifth inning. Chrissie, Moondance, and Evans all grounded out to the pitcher, so we didn't score. In the bottom of the fifth Frank walked the first three guys up. Then the next ball got hit to Brian. Brian threw the ball to Mop and we got the runner coming in from third base. Then they had two new kids who I had never seen play before. They were huge and they were twins.

"These kids on your roster?" Marla asked the Hawks' coach.

◆ 117

"Sure," he said, "they were just out of town for a while."

The first kid gets up and hits a line drive right to Brian. That ball was hit so hard, even I jumped. Brian caught it, but I saw him rub his hand afterward.

I backed up at third.

The other kid, the first big kid's twin, struck out. It was still 8 to 3 with one more inning to go.

"Hey, you see those big kids they got?" Evans asked Marla.

"I'd like to see if they were really on his roster from the beginning of the season," Marla said.

"They looked like the monster twins from the Planet Ugly!" Chrissie said.

"That's the first smart thing I've ever heard you say," Brian said.

"You think that's what they look like?" Chrissie asked. She had this little smile on her face again.

"Exactly," Brian said.

"That's because you probably come from there too," Chrissie said, putting on a batting helmet.

Brian went after Chrissie, but Marla got to him before he got to Chrissie. They argued some more, but I wasn't watching them. Mop was pointing at the fence down near the foul line. I looked and saw Peaches leaning on the top of the fence. He waved to me and I waved back.

"If he disappeared, it looks like he didn't disappear long," I said to Mop.

"I don't see no llama with him," she said.

I didn't either.

I was up first in the sixth and got a hit. It was a slow

roller right through the first baseman's legs. I had put a lot of English on that ball. I got to second base so fast it wasn't even funny. Mr. Treaster was yelling something at the umpire. Then they threw the ball to first base and said I was out. They said I hadn't stepped on first base. I guess they were right because nobody on my team argued about it.

Lo Vinh pinch-hit for Joey and struck out. Then Frank struck out, got mad, and threw his bat all the way across the field. That's why they put him out of the game and Jennifer had to play.

"Okay, now they're trying everything in the book to get us to lose this game," Marla said. "The Eagles must be pretty worried if their coach is here trying to help another team beat us. Let's just hold them for this one inning, and we're in the play-offs! Okay, let's do it!"

Boy, I was really mad at that Treaster. He kept on talking to Evans, who was playing first base, trying to make him mad. You can make Evans mad easy and then he makes errors.

Lo Vinh was pitching and the first Hawk got up and hit a ground ball to Brian. Brian got it and threw it to Evans, but it bounced on the ground first and hit Evans on the leg. Evans picked it up and tagged the bag just before their guy got there. One out.

The next guy hit a fly ball to Moondance and he caught it. Just like it was nothing. He just stood under that ball and caught it the way they do on television. I don't know how come he's my brother and he can do it like that.

One more out and I was hoping they didn't hit it to me.

"There's a hard smash down third-base line!" Mike

was announcing the game again. "T.J. dives for it! It goes off his arm! Now it goes off his chest! Now it's rolling around!"

"He ain't running!" I could hear Evans screeching from across the field. I looked up from the ball. The Hawk batter was still standing in the batter's box.

"That's a foul ball!" he called out.

"Fair ball!" The umpire was standing right next to me.

"T.J. picks it up!" Mike was standing almost on top of me shouting in my ear. "The long throw to first . . . Out!" That was me. I did it.

We all had to line up and shake the other team's hand the way you do after every game. You don't really shake hands. You kind of slap their hands. Brian wanted to be the first in line and then run to the back of the line so he could do it again, but Marla wouldn't let him.

"You scouting us?" Marla asked Mr. Treaster when he came over.

"You got two ball players on that team," he said. "That Brian kid and the girl behind the plate. You can't beat us with just two players."

"Then you didn't have to be here to watch us, did you?" Marla said.

Mr. Treaster turned on his heel and walked away without looking back.

"What's wrong with him?" Chrissie asked.

"I don't know," Marla said. "Maybe it's what's right with us."

"Hey, here comes that weird friend of yours, T.J.," Brian said, poking me in the side.

I looked up and saw Peaches headed our way. I started

to speak to him but he went right past me and up to Marla.

"Sister Carmelita said that one of your pitchers needed a little help pitching close to people," Peaches said. "I think maybe I can help him."

Marla looked at Moondance, then at me, and then she turned and looked to where Mr. Treaster was just getting into his car.

"What did you have in mind?" she asked.

wo big trucks came on Wednesday and moved some stuff from the Academy. They took all the desks from the third-floor classrooms, and all the blackboards. There were only fourteen kids left at the Academy and late Wednesday the four youngest went in a station wagon to Little Flower in Riverhead.

Me and Moondance were there when they were packing the kids' things and getting them in the car. Sister Marianne said it was good that the older kids came back to help the younger ones. Another kid, Keith, had come back to help with the packing too. I didn't like him when he was at the Academy and he still wasn't too cool.

"You guys like your new parents?" he asked.

"Yeah, they're nice," I said. "Only they're not new anymore."

"Mine are okay," he said. "They're kind of corny, though."

"All parents are corny," Moondance said. "That's part of their job."

"At least we got adopted," Keith said, nodding toward Mop.

I just walked away from Keith. Mop was my friend, and nothing in the world was going to change that, ever. It seemed when nobody else in the whole world wanted or cared for us, we wanted and cared for each other, and things like that just didn't go away so easy.

I went over to where she was getting the kids settled in the back of the station wagon that was going to take them out to Little Flower, their new home.

"Don't cry, Moppy," one of the kids was saying. "You can go next time. Okay?"

"Sure," Mop nodded and looked away, but not before I saw her red eyes and the tears on her face.

I rubbed her shoulder. I don't know why, but I did, and she jerked it away.

She went upstairs before the station wagon left.

"I imagine you boys are going to stay around for dessert tonight," Sister Marianne said.

"No, I don't think so," I said.

"T.J." Sister Marianne took my hands in hers. "I know you're sad about the Academy closing."

I looked at her and there were tears in her eyes too.

"A little," I said.

"Just remember that the Lord works in mysterious ways"—she sniffed twice—"His wonders to perform."

Sister Carmelita came into the office we were in, saw Sister Marianne, and turned sharply around.

"Sister Carmelita!" Sister Marianne's voice was so loud, it made Moondance jump.

Sister Carmelita came back into the room. Mop was waiting outside in the hallway. I looked at her and she turned away. I figured she was still crying.

"You know the Little League season is almost over," Sister Carmelita said, quickly putting the catching mitt behind her back. "There are only a few more practices left . . ."

"I suppose it's better than sitting around here moping about the Academy's closing," Sister Marianne said. "As a matter of fact, I might even join you for today's practice."

"That would not be a good idea," Sister Carmelita said. "Moondance has to practice his pitching and he might not be able to concentrate with you there."

"If he can concentrate with all of those children and parents screaming at him from the sidelines, I'm sure that he can concentrate with me just watching him practice," Sister Marianne said, taking her wallet and keys from the desk.

Sister Carmelita looked up toward the ceiling. "With all due respect, Sister, he's used to those children and the parents. You always said that we had to make a difference in the lives of the young people at the Academy. And you're a lot different from the others. . . ."

Sister Marianne looked at Sister Carmelita for a long while and then put her keys and wallet down on the desk. "If you say so. . . ." she said.

In a minute Sister Carmelita had us all out and headed down the street.

We went down toward the park and then Sister Carmelita had us stand near the entrance while she checked back to see if anyone was watching us. Then she scooted us across the street toward Bergen Avenue.

"What are we going down here for?" Mop asked.

"You'll see."

"Where's Marla?" I asked.

"Waiting for us."

We went down Bergen until we got to Goodman's, an old abandoned department store. It was boarded over and there were graffiti all over the walls. Sister Carmelita looked quickly around, and then opened one of the side doors.

The inside of the store was spooky and Sister Carmelita stopped and put her hand across my chest.

"Mrs. Kennedy?"

"Here!" Marla's voice called out.

We went forward a little and then a light came on in the back of the store. Sister Carmelita went first and we followed close behind her.

When we got to the back of the store, we saw that the light was in another room. We went in and saw Marla fixing something on the floor. Peaches was standing near a rack.

"Moondance, come over here," she said.

Moondance went over to where the coach was kneeling.

"This is your pitching position," Marla said. "Mop, get down there to where Peaches is standing. That's home plate."

"Go on," Sister Carmelita said. "Warm up."

Moondance looked at me. I shrugged. I didn't know what was going on either.

He threw the ball a few times to Mop. Nothing special. He was too busy looking around the old store. There were racks and counters, and even an old cash register with the drawers open.

"You can throw harder than that, Moondance," Marla said.

Zip! Whick.

Zip! Whick.

Zip. Whick.

That's how it sounded. Moondance kept looking around the store. I guess he was wondering why we were practicing in there instead of in the park. I know I was.

Zip. Whick.

"This here is where I stay sometime when it be raining out," Peaches said.

Zip. Whick.

Zip. Whick.

The ball went straight over the plate into Mop's glove.

"How's he doing, Mop?" Marla asked.

"Pretty good," Mop said.

"You think he's ready for Babe Ruth yet?" Peaches asked.

"I think so," Marla said.

Peaches went behind one of the counters and came out with a dummy. It was the kind of dummy you see modeling clothes. Only Peaches had him dressed up in a baseball uniform and had a bat taped to his arms so he looked as if he could be batting.

"Must be an Eagle." Mop rubbed her nose with the palm of her hand. "He sure looks dumb."

"Let's see you pitch to him," Marla said to Moondance.

"If he gets a hit, you're off the team," Mop said.

Moondance was smiling. He wound up and threw the ball.

Zip! Right across the floor of the department store. It had to be a mile outside.

"Okay," Marla said. "You don't want to hit the dummy. But you know you can't hurt him so we're going to keep practicing until you can throw the ball closer."

Moondance threw the ball again, but he was still outside with the pitch.

"Slow it down a little," Peaches said.

Moondance threw the ball slower and it went over.

"There you go!"

He kept pitching, each time throwing just a little harder. The ball was still going outside a lot, but he was coming closer.

"Aw, you can't pitch!" Sister Carmelita called out.

Moondance looked over at her.

"Ignore the crowd, Moondance," Marla said. "Just concentrate on your pitching."

Zip! Whack! Right over!

"It looked like a ball to me!" Sister Carmelita had her hands cupped around her mouth and sounded as if she were a long way away.

Moondance smiled.

Zip! Whack!

Zip! Whack!

"Just think about Mop's glove," Marla said.

Zip! Whack!

"Think about Mop's hand too," Mop said.

"You okay, baby?" Marla put her hand up to stop Moondance from throwing the ball.

"You kidding me?" Mop said. "I don't hurt that easy, and I ain't your baby!"

Marla took a deep breath, let it out slowly. Then told Moondance to pitch again.

Zip! Whack!

Zip! Whack!

Then there was another noise. It sounded like something banging on the ground. I looked at Marla.

"I don't hear anything!" Sister Carmelita said. She put both hands over her ears.

"Pitch, Moondance." Marla folded her arms and watched my brother.

Zip! Whack!

Zip! Whack!

Then there was the other sound again. There was the banging and then a soft little noise. When we heard that soft noise, something between a bark and a moo, we knew what it was.

I looked over at Marla and she looked up at the ceiling. I looked over at Peaches and he pointed behind a counter at the back of the store.

Mop got there first and by the time Moondance and I reached the counter, she had both of her arms around Taffy's neck. She was tied to a small pipe and there was a bowl of vegetables near her. Taffy was humming.

"How long has she been here?" Moondance asked.

"That's not the question," Peaches asked. "The question is, what are we going to do with her?"

"We'll think of something," Marla said. "Now we have to get back to our practice. That is, if anyone here is interested in beating the Eagles this Friday."

The rest of the practice went okay. Sometimes Moon-dance would pitch outside, but he got a lot more of the balls over the plate. He looked like he was going to be okay.

he play-offs! It was us against the Eagles. Whoever won two out of the three games would be the champions of the league.

The first game was on a Friday, and it was one of those just perfect days. There wasn't a cloud in the sky. Dad came home early to watch the game. I wasn't too happy about that, but I guess it was okay. Moondance pitched.

The whole game was like a dream. The Eagles were up first and they didn't score. Then we got up and we didn't score. That was the way the game went for four innings. Then, in the fifth inning, they got two hits in a row. One guy got a single and Rocky hit the ball against the fence. They scored one run and then their next batter struck out. The score was 1 to 0.

Taisha was on the sideline biting her nails. She was too nervous to cheer.

In our half of the fifth inning we didn't score.

In the sixth inning they got their first two batters on base. Then they tried a double steal and Mop threw out the guy going to second. The next guy popped up to Evans on first, and the last guy struck out.

We got up in the bottom of the sixth. Their best pitcher, David Babar, was pitching. Joey DeLea got a single. Then Frank struck out, and Mop grounded out to first base. Joey DeLea went to second on Mop's ground-out and it was all up to Brian. He hit the first ball as hard as he could and the ball went flying toward the outfield.

Their center fielder kept backing up and backing up. Then, at the last minute, he jumped and caught the ball. Brian was already past second base, but it was no use. It was the third out. We had lost the game.

Miserable. That's how everybody felt. Moondance had pitched well. We had only given up one run. *One* run, and we had still lost.

We were supposed to play the next game Saturday, but it rained for three days straight. Then the game was canceled the next day because the field was too muddy.

When we did play, Marla had Brian pitching.

We got up first and Joey DeLea hit the first ball into center field for a base hit. Then Frank walked and Mop struck out. Brian struck out, too, and all the Eagles were glad to see that. Mike missed the first two pitches and the next pitch hit him. He went to first base and the bases were loaded. But Chrissie was up.

The Eagles' third-base guy moved in and Rocky moved in from first base.

"Let her hit it!" Mr. Treaster was calling.

The first pitch was high, but the umpire called it a strike anyway. Marla kicked some dirt with her foot.

The next pitch was high, too, but Chrissie swung and knocked it over the second baseman's head into center field! Joey and Frank both scored. It was the first time that Chrissie had ever got a swinging hit.

Her brothers were going crazy on the sidelines and all the Elks were screaming.

Moondance made the last out. Their pitcher made a good play and stopped a hard ground ball. But that was okay, we had scored two runs!

We stayed two runs ahead until the third inning. In the third inning Rocky hit a ball that went over the right-field fence. It was 2 to 1.

In the fifth inning Brian walked a batter and then Rocky hit the next pitch over the center-field fence and the score was 3 to 2, their favor.

They all gave Rocky high-fives when he went into their dugout and they thought they had the game won. So did we.

In the sixth inning Frank was up first and was thrown out at first. Then Mop got a single and Brian came up. Their outfielders started backing up and I was just hoping that Brian would smack one. I thought he would. I could almost feel it.

Marla called time out and went and talked to Brian.

Brian nodded and went up to the plate. He put the bat between his legs and spit on his hands. Man, he looked so good it was wonderful. Then the pitcher threw the ball and Brian bunted. When the bat hit the ball, the first thing the third baseman did was to back up, that's how sure he was that Brian was going to smash that ball. By the time he saw it was a bunt, Brian was on first base and Mop was on second.

"I don't believe it! I don't believe it!" Mr. Treaster was screaming at the top of his lungs. "She has the best hitter on the team bunting!"

He started laughing and the Eagles started shaking their heads as if it was some kind of a big joke or something. Mike was due up next, but Marla put in Jennifer to bat for him. Mr. Treaster was really laughing and all the Eagles were pointing at Jennifer.

Marla called Jennifer over to the batting cage.

"This pitcher throws the ball high," Marla said. "He doesn't throw very hard, either. Just meet the ball with the bat."

"If she hits it, she's too fat to run!" Rocky called out from first base.

I felt like running over and punching him in the face.

The first pitch was over and Jennifer didn't swing.

"Strike one!"

Marla wiped her hands on her pants. She was nervous too.

The next pitch was over.

"Strike two!"

Jennifer turned and looked at the umpire.

"She don't wanna swing!" Mr. Treaster called down to Jennifer.

The next pitch was high and Jennifer swung. The ball went out toward center field. The second baseman ran out and the center fielder ran in. The ball dropped right between them.

Mop scored easily. Brian came around third base just as the center fielder got the ball. The center fielder threw the ball to the second baseman and the second baseman threw a bullet right to their catcher. Brian and the ball reached the catcher at the same time. No contest. Brian knocked the catcher down and we were ahead.

We didn't score any more runs. We were ahead 4 to 3.

Their first batter hit a soft grounder to Evans. He took the ball and stepped on first. One out.

The second batter hit a ground ball to Brian. Brian threw the ball to Evans at first. Two outs.

The next two batters walked. Then Brian hit the next guy with a pitch. The bases were loaded and guess who was at bat?

Marla called time out and switched me and Jennifer. I was going to play right field and Jennifer was coming in to play third base.

"They won't have him bunting, I'm sure," Marla said.

From where I stood in the outfield, home plate seemed a thousand miles away. I watched as Brian wound up and started to pitch.

Crack!

Rocky hit a high fly ball. I could tell it was coming toward me. All of a sudden I couldn't breathe. I couldn't move. I couldn't do anything. The ball came down so slowly. I backed up a little.

I don't pray to God to catch a ball or anything like that. They say that you shouldn't pray for little things like catching a ball. You shouldn't.

I kept backing up.

The ball got faster as it came down. And faster. And faster. And all of a sudden it was dropping in front of me. I reached out at the last minute and felt it hit my glove.

Then I looked on the ground for the ball and I didn't see it. I turned and looked behind me, but it wasn't there either. I lifted my hands and there, in the webbing of my glove, was the ball. I had caught it! I had caught it!

The whole team jumped on me. They were screaming in my ears. Marla was banging me on the back and Jennifer was shaking me. Brian had his arm around my neck so hard, I could hardly breathe, but it didn't matter. I had caught the ball! The Elks had won!

We were really up when we took the field for practice the next day. Some of the Eagles came around and watched us and made a lot of stupid comments. But they weren't that stupid anymore, because we had finally won a game from them.

When we were finished, the Eagles took the field. I watched them for a while and saw that they could do two things really good. They could catch good and they could curse good.

The Eagles cursed more than any team in the league. But the funny thing was that the cursing seemed to help them win games. Everybody was a little afraid of them. They seemed older than the rest of us.

Mr. Treaster was good at yelling. He yelled at everybody on his team except Rocky. I guess you didn't fool around on Mr. Treaster's team.

When we were leaving the field, Mr. Treaster came over and asked Marla who was pitching in the final game.

"Williams," she said. "Number Twenty-one."

"Yeah, I saw him in the first game," Mr. Treaster said. "That's quite a combination, that Williams boy and your little girl catcher."

"We hope so," Marla said, and walked away from him.

I liked that. The way she spoke to him and then just walked away like it didn't mean a lot when it really did.

After everyone had gone home, Marla took me, Moondance, and Mop back to the old department store. Moondance practiced pitching against that dummy again.

Zip! Whack!

Zip! Whack!

The ball flew over the plate, just inches from the dummy. I looked over at Marla and she looked at me and smiled. Moondance was good. Real good.

The last game. Whoever won would be the league champion. Moondance was going to pitch and everybody was nervous. Fifteen minutes before game time and Lo Vinh hadn't shown up, Evans hadn't shown up, and Chrissie's mom had called Marla and said that she was sick and wouldn't be coming to the game.

Everybody else came, though. I mean everybody else in the entire world. Sister Marianne brought some of the kids from the Academy, the ones that hadn't gone out to Riverhead yet. Peaches and Miss Sally brought some of their friends, and some guy came from the mayor's office. That was lucky for us because Mr. Treaster wanted the game forfeited when we didn't have enough players at game time.

Brian's mother had brought a cooler full of lemonade, but Marla said that we weren't to have any before the third inning.

"I want you all to drink plenty of water before the game," she said.

We weren't that thirsty, but all of us had to go to the bathroom. Even Taisha.

The guy from the mayor's office said that the mayor would show up any moment and not to start the game before he got there.

"You *are* playing in a city park," the guy said.

Treaster smiled but he wasn't happy. The mayor showed up just when Evans did. And by the time a woman from the *Journal* had taken pictures of the mayor and everything, Lo Vinh had shown up and Chrissie, too. Her mother said that she had been so nervous before the game that she had thrown up. I can't even imagine Chrissie being nervous.

The Eagles were up first and Moondance threw strikes right past them. One—two—three.

The Elks were cheering like crazy. I looked at Marla and she was smiling away. I looked over at Mr. Treaster. He wasn't standing in front of the Eagles' dugout the way he usually did. He was standing to one side talking to a guy in a suit.

The bottom half of the first inning and Joey, Frank, and Mop all made outs in the same way, ground balls back to the pitcher. Now the Eagles were cheering. Marla still looked like she thought we were going to win and Mr. Treaster was still standing off to one side talking to the guy in the suit.

The Eagles got up in the second inning and Rocky got a double, but the next three guys made outs.

When we took the field, the mayor came out and said how wonderful it was that we were all playing baseball and that the Little League was making America great. He didn't say how it was making America great, just that it was. Then he left. That's when the trouble started.

Moondance made the first pitch. It was a strike. Then the guy in the suit came over and spoke to the umpire behind the plate. He was pointing at Mop. Marla went over to see what was going on. The umpire behind the plate shrugged and came over to the umpire who was on third base. That's how I heard what they were talking about.

"This guy's from the Children's Welfare Association," the home plate umpire was saying. "He says that they shouldn't have a girl catching."

"And just why not?" Marla asked.

"Because her body weight might not be able to take the heat of the day and the heat generated by the catcher's equipment," the guy said. "He thinks that it's wrong for anyone to have a young girl catching on a day like this."

Marla's lips were moving, but nothing came out.

"I can catch!" Mop said.

"What do you say?" Marla asked the umpire.

"There's nothing in Little League rules that make differences between boys and girls," the umpire said. "So I guess it's up to you."

Marla looked at Mr. Treaster and then at Mop. She called Evans over from first base and Frank in from the outfield.

She told Evans to catch, put Frank on first, and Mop in the outfield. Mop was mad and started to argue with Marla.

"Either play where you're told or I'll bring in another player," Marla said.

Marla turned on her heel and started back to the dugout.

"I thought she liked me." Mop was pounding her fist into her old fielder's glove.

"I think she does," I said.

"She sure has a funny way of showing it," Brian said. You could smell trouble.

Moondance pitched again to the first guy. He popped up and Brian caught it. The next guy walked. Then he stole second when Evans missed Moondance's pitch.

"Throw the ball straight!" Evans chirped from behind the catcher's mask.

The ball had been straight, but Evans had just missed it.

The batter struck out, but not before the runner stole third. He scored on a groundout. The next guy struck out. We were behind by one run.

Dave Babar wasn't that good a pitcher, but he was good enough. He got our side out in the bottom of the second.

Moondance settled down in the third and struck out the three guys he faced.

In our side of the third we went down just as easily. Zip!

Moondance's first pitch was right over the plate. Evans missed it but it didn't mean too much because nobody was on base. The next pitch got hit on the fly to Joey DeLea. Joey caught it and there was one out. The next batter bunted to me. I picked it up and threw it to Mike at first base. The ball bounced in front of Mike, then he kicked it back over toward Moondance and the runner was safe.

The runner took off on the first pitch and Evans threw the ball into center field. The runner came around second base and slid into third.

"We're going to kill you guys," he said as he dusted himself off.

"You're going to get killed!" I said.

"Not by you, you little punk!" He bumped into me on purpose. "Rocky beat you and your brother up. We're thinking about beating the crap out of your whole team!"

"Look alive, T.J.!" Marla called out to me.

"Hey, what's T.J. stand for?" a kid from the Eagles yelled. "Turkey Juice?"

The next ball was a line drive right to me. It hit my glove and then my chest, and then knocked my cap off.

"First! First!"

I heard Jennifer's voice from the bench. I went after the ball, got it near the pitcher's mound, and threw it to first. Out! But the runner had scored. It was 2 to 0.

Mop, Brian, and Mike struck out in the bottom of the fourth. The top of the fifth inning came and their first batter, a skinny kid named Benny, hit the ball really hard. The ball went all the way to the fence and Benny, who was kind of slow, ended up on second base. Moondance looked over at me. He looked miserable. Marla called time out and motioned for Mop to come in from the outfield.

Mop came trotting in and Mr. Treaster started talking to the guy in the suit again.

"Look, Mop." Marla knelt down. "You're the best catcher we've got. We can't let them score any more runs."

"Then how come you stuck me in the outfield?" Mop asked.

"Because I'm not sure if this character in the suit is right or not," Marla said. "And I just don't want to do anything wrong with you."

"Yeah, but don't you want to win the game?" Mop asked. *"Don't you?"*

"I want to win so bad I could spit!" Marla said.

"So spit while I get my catching stuff on."

"There's a problem," Marla said. "If this guy is really from the Children's Welfare Association and he's right about girls catching when it's too hot, he might give me trouble . . . later on."

"Hey, Marla, you're on my side, ain't you?" Mop said. "Don't we make a cool team and everything?"

"Hey, c'mon!" Treaster shouted across the field. "Let's get this show on the road!"

"Mop." Marla put her hands on Mop's shoulders. "We make a very cool team."

"So fight for me," Mop said, strapping on the shin guards. "I'm worth it."

The guy in the suit came over to Marla and asked if she was going to let Mop catch again.

"Not only am I going to let her catch," Marla said, "but if you don't get off the field I'm going to break your kneecaps!"

The guy puffed up and turned a little red. Then he

whipped out a notebook, wrote something down in it, and stormed off to the Eagles' side of the field.

Evans went back to first base and Frank went to the outfield.

Zip! Whack!

Zip! Whack!

Zip! Whack!

Moondance struck out three batters in a row.

We were still down 2 to 0. Evans started off the last of the fifth by popping up. I was up next and I hit the first pitch over the left-field fence. It was my best hit ever in my entire life. It was just a little foul, though. That was the first strike. The second ball I hit a hard smash down the left-field line. That was a little foul too. The next pitch looked a little too low.

"Strike threeeee! You're out!"

I was sure that umpire couldn't see too good. That ball had to be low by at least six inches, or maybe three.

Joey hit a ball straight up in the air. He thought it was going to be foul. So did I. It wasn't and their catcher threw him out.

Moondance got their first two batters in the top of the sixth. Then their next batter walked. Then Rocky got up. Mop went out to talk to Moondance, and me and Evans went over to see what they were talking about.

"Stay close to that guy on first base so he don't steal," Mop told Evans.

"Don't tell me how to play first base," Evans came back.

"Okay, break it up," the umpire said.

Rocky hit a hard foul ball right past the third-base coach.

"Straighten it out, Rocky!" Mr. Treaster was clapping his hands.

The next pitch was way outside, but Mop got it quickly and threw it to Evans. The runner went sliding back into the base.

"You're out!" The umpire jerked his hand in the air. It was almost as if the umpire had a string in his hand that was tied to Mr. Treaster, because just as the umpire's hand went up Mr. Treaster jumped into the air.

"You gotta be kidding! You gotta be kidding!" Mr. Treaster turned red. "He was safe by a mile!"

"He's out!" the umpire repeated.

Mop had picked him off!

Bottom of the sixth. We were still losing by two runs. Mr. Treaster calmed down a little and started telling his players that all they needed was three more outs.

"Just three more turkeys to shoot down," he said.

"C'mon guys." Marla was clapping her hands together. "Let's do it!"

"You can do it!" Taisha was shaking my arm. "You can do it!"

The crowd on their side of the field was making a ton of noise and then the crowd on our side of the field started making a ton of noise and you couldn't even hear yourself think.

Frank got up first and hit a ball that stayed right at home plate. Frank ran while their catcher picked it up and threw it to first. It hit Frank instead and rolled away. Frank started to cry, the way he always did when something went wrong, and said he wanted to go home, but Marla told him to go stay on first because she needed him in the outfield in case we tied the game up.

Mop had two strikes and then hit a slow ground ball to the shortstop. The guy came running in, grabbed the ball with one hand, and threw it to Rocky at first base. The shortstop made a great play, but Rocky dropped the ball and Mop was safe!

Brian hit his first ball right over their second baseman's head. It went into the outfield and all the way to the fence. Frank scored and Mop stayed at third. Brian was on second and the score was 2 to 1.

Mike struck out. Then he threw his helmet down, which automatically put him out of the game.

Chrissie was up next. Marla called her over and talked to her. The Eagles brought their infield in. On the first pitch Chrissie swung and missed by a mile.

"Come on, Chrissie," Marla called to her. "You can hit, I know you can!"

The Eagles moved their infield back a little on the next pitch. Chrissie bunted the ball to Rocky at first base. He fielded the ball, looked at Mop going home, and decided to tag first base instead. Mop scored and the game was tied!

Brian had moved to third base.

Mr. Treaster called time out. He went out and talked to the pitcher. I could see him pointing toward first base and then toward Brian at third.

"What's he telling him?" Jennifer asked Marla.

"Probably not to give Moondance anything too good to swing at," Marla said. "They can afford to walk a batter, but they can't let Brian score or we win the game and the play-offs."

Marla was right. Moondance was up and he walked on four straight pitches.

Evans couldn't find his batting helmet and the game was held up while he looked for it. Mr. Treaster told the umpire that Evans should be out if he didn't come to bat, but the umpire didn't say anything. Then, after Evans still couldn't find his helmet, the umpire told the pitcher to pitch to an empty plate. The pitcher started winding up just when Evans saw that Jennifer was sitting on his helmet.

"Strike one!" the umpire called.

"Come on, Evans," Marla yelled "Get up!"

"Jennifer was trying to hatch my helmet!" Evans gave Jennifer a dirty look.

He stepped into the batter's box, then looked over at Jennifer again.

"Strike two!"

"Pay attention, Evans!" Marla yelled.

"She caused them strikes!" Evans yelled back.

The next pitch was over Evans's head, but he swung anyway and hit a ground ball to the Eagles' third baseman. He grabbed it on one bounce and made a diving leap to tag Brian, who was off the bag. Brian jumped over the tag and made it back to third base. Evans made it to first base.

"The bases are loaded!" Jennifer screamed. "Who's up?"

"T.J.!"

"Let's go, T.J.!" Our whole bench was chanting. "Let's go!"

I didn't want to get up.

"He can't hit!" Rocky called out from first base. "He's a big nothing!"

As soon as I stepped into the batter's box the pitcher wound up and threw the ball. It came right at me and I jumped back out of the way.

"Strike one!" the umpire called.

"Come on, T.J.," Mop was screaming. "Kill it!"

The next pitch came and I moved just a little because it was inside.

"Strike two!"

"One more! One more!" Mr. Treaster yelled out to the pitcher. "This kid's afraid of the ball."

"Stay in there, T.J.!" Marla called out. "You can do it!"

Mr. Treaster was right. I *was* afraid of the ball hitting me. I gripped the bat as tight as I could and stared at the pitcher. He wound up and pitched the ball. I didn't want to move away from the ball. I didn't want to close my eyes either, but I did.

Phoop! Right in the back. That's where the ball hit me. Marla came running over and the umpire grabbed me.

"You okay?"

"Yeah," I said. My back hurt where the ball hit me, but I said I was okay anyway.

"You're on first!" The umpire pointed to me.

"We win! We win!"

Jennifer was screaming. The Elks were jumping up and down. I went to first base and Brian came in to score. We had won the play-offs!

We got our trophies on that Wednesday night. It was the first trophy I had ever won. There was a little statue of a guy on top and on the bottom, on a brass plate, it read *Elks, Lincoln Park League Champions.* Brian got two trophies. One was the same as we all got and the other was Most Valuable Player. Dad said that if they had a trophy for most improved player, I would have gotten it. I didn't think that was true, though. I mean, I was pretty good to begin with, so how could I improve that much?

It didn't change me just because I became a champion. No one on the team changed except Mop. She changed something terrible.

She used to be the toughest girl I ever knew. If you went up to her and said something she didn't like, she might take a swing at you. Pow! Just like that! After we won the championship, she changed completely. Or maybe it was after the Academy signed the papers and she went home with Marla and Jim. She was adopted at last. Or maybe it was when she found out how much Marla really liked her.

"I thought Mom was scouting me to see how good I could play," Mop said. We were in Marla's house, Mop's

house too, now, and watching television until Marla got ready to go with us to the Academy.

"You gonna tell us the same thing again?" Moondance asked.

"I just thought it was far out that she was coaching because she was scared she couldn't get along with me," Mop said. "And all the time I couldn't even talk to her because I thought I couldn't get along with her."

"You already said that three times," Moondance said.

"Well, don't you think we're just alike?"

"Nope." I pushed the button on the remote control and watched as the Bionic Six disappeared and the Transformers showed up on the screen.

"That's 'cause you can't see nothing!" Mop said. "We're just alike."

"Did you see Treaster when Marla took the team trophy?" I asked. "I thought he was going to break his face trying to get a smile going."

"Yeah, and you see that smile Mom gave him back?" Mop asked.

"You like saying those words, like *Mom* and *Dad,*" I said. "You're always saying them."

"I got that from you, Bright Eyes," Mop said with a big grin.

Mop's new parents were ready and we left. My folks were going to meet us at the Academy. I knew I wouldn't get to talk too much to Mop that evening. That's how she's changed. Ever since she's been adopted she acts different. When Marla comes around—when Mop's mom comes around—Mop just wants to hold her hand

and stuff like that. I can't even imagine Mop doing that in the old days at the Academy.

The reason we were all going to the Academy was that it was Sister Marianne's last day. The Sisters of Charity were transferring her to another position and Sister Carmelita was giving her a farewell party. Father Magnus was there, Brian, Chrissie, me, Mop, and Moondance from the Elks and some of the other nuns and also some of the parents who had adopted kids. Sister Carmelita had invited Peaches too.

"We're not here to honor Sister Marianne," Sister Carmelita said. "All of her good works over the years are her honors, and all the happy children we see before us are her awards."

Everybody clapped and some of the people stood up. Then Sister Marianne spoke.

"Leaving any place one loves is a little sad," she said. "But I really have mixed feelings about leaving the Academy. I'm pleased that it will stay open as a day care center, but I'm not sure if I like being replaced by a llama. As you know, the archdiocese has decided that we can keep Taffy as a companion for the children."

"And the mayor promised to provide support for her," Father Magnus added.

"Probably trying to line up the llama vote," Sister Marianne said. "I'm also glad that I was here long enough to see the stained-glass window replaced. It was broken seven years ago, a week before I came here, and I've been trying to get money to fix it all these years."

"I was in high school when it broke," Sister Carmelita said.

"That's when she was really a pitcher," Dad said.

"I'd like to see you pitch sometime." Brian's whole mouth was covered with chocolate crumbs.

"I'm afraid not," Sister Carmelita said.

"How come?" Moondance asked. "Mop's glove and ball and things are still here."

"Sister Carmelita has dedicated herself to higher things," Sister Marianne said. "There's a chance that one day she'll be in complete charge of the Academy. She'll be doing work just a wee bit more associated with His will and she'll have to keep her mind there."

"She gonna do a fine job, too." Peaches looked good in a suit and bow tie.

"Lastly, I have a word for our Little Leaguers." Sister Marianne looked over at us. "Even though I'm not a lover of baseball, I would like to congratulate you young people and you, Mrs. Kennedy, on your victory."

"Thank you," Marla said.

"T.J. got the winning hit in the last game," Brian said. "Only the ball hit him instead of him hitting the ball!"

"You'd be surprised what you have to do to be a champion sometimes," Marla said.

"The whole parish was proud that some of our Academy children were on the Elks," Sister Marianne said. "Did you see the write-up the parish paper gave the team?"

"Is it in the parish paper?" Sister Carmelita stood up. "I'll get it."

"I have it in my office," Sister Marianne said. "I can get it. I'm not that old yet."

"We were in the *Journal*, too," Brian said as Sister

Marianne started for the paper. "They've got a picture of Moondance striking out somebody."

"Were you really a great pitcher?" Moondance asked.

"Would you like to see how I pitch?" Sister Carmelita glanced over her shoulder at the door Sister Marianne had gone through.

"Sure," I said.

"Yeah." Moondance wiped at his face with his sleeve.

"Mop, get the glove."

Mop went, grabbed her glove, tossed a ball to Sister Carmelita, and crouched down.

"Go on, Titi." Dad hit his palm with his fist. "Throw one in there for old times' sake."

Sister Carmelita leaned forward and Mop gave her the signal for a fastball. Sister Carmelita rocked back, turned, and threw the ball.

It was really fast! And really high!

The stained-glass pane didn't actually break, it just cracked where the ball hit it.

"I'm out of here!" Brian grabbed for his coat.

"You sit down, Brian!" Mop said, throwing her glove on top of a small closet.

Everybody sat back down and tried to look innocent. Only Brian was laughing when Sister Marianne came back into the room.

"Here's the write-up—" she said, then she looked at all of us sitting so still and squinched her face up. "This looks like quite an important conversation, is it something you can share with me?"

"Sister Carmelita was just convincing us of the need

for the community to join together in meeting the church's needs," Dad said.

"Sister Carmelita was doing this?" Sister Marianne looked at Sister Carmelita and smiled. "Well, they say the Lord works in mysterious ways—"

"His wonders to perform," Mop said.

Dad and some other people helped Sister Carmelita get the windowpane replaced. But things didn't really get back to normal until Mop met Rocky in the A&P and Rocky called her a freckle-faced monkey. Mop told me that if the guy who fixes the vegetables hadn't stopped her, she would have torn Rocky's head right off his shoulders. She probably would have, too.

Anyway, I'm glad she's back to normal. We've got one more year on the Elks, and good catchers are hard to find.

About the Author

Walter Dean Myers is the author of many books for young readers, including *Mr. Monkey and the Gotcha Bird*, *Hoops*, an American Library Association Best Book for Young Adults, and its sequel, *The Outside Shot*.

Walter Dean Myers lives in Jersey City, New Jersey.